'Why d[...] stand[...] with the candle in her hand, with her cruel contemptuous eyes fixed on me, and the glittering serpent, like a familiar demon, o[...]

GEORGE ELIOT
Born 1819, Warwickshire, England
Died 1880, London, England

Eliot wrote the essay 'Silly Novels by Lady Novelists' for the *Westminster Review* in October 1856. She wrote 'The Lifted Veil' in early 1859, while working on her novel *The Mill on the Floss*. It was published in *Blackwood's Edinburgh Magazine* in July of that year.

ELIOT IN PENGUIN CLASSICS
Scenes of Clerical Life
Adam Bede
The Mill on the Floss
Silas Marner
Romola
Felix Holt, the Radical
Middlemarch
Daniel Deronda
Selected Essays, Poems and Other Writings

GEORGE ELIOT

The Lifted Veil

PENGUIN BOOKS

PENGUIN CLASSICS

UK | USA | Canada | Ireland | Australia
India | New Zealand | South Africa

Penguin Classics is part of the Penguin Random House group of companies
whose addresses can be found at global.penguinrandomhouse.com.

This edition published in Penguin Classics 2016
001

Set in 9.5/13 pt Baskerville 10 Pro
Typeset by Jouve (UK), Milton Keynes
Printed in Great Britain by Clays Ltd, St Ives plc

A CIP catalogue record for this book is available from the British Library

ISBN: 978–0–241–25123–2

www.greenpenguin.co.uk

Penguin Random House is committed to a
sustainable future for our business, our readers
and our planet. This book is made from Forest
Stewardship Council® certified paper.

Contents

THE LIFTED VEIL

Give me no light, great Heaven, but such as turns
To energy of human fellowship;
No powers beyond the growing heritage
That makes completer manhood.

Chapter 1

The time of my end approaches. I have lately been subject to attacks of *angina pectoris;* and in the ordinary course of things, my physician tells me, I may fairly hope that my life will not be protracted many months. Unless, then, I am cursed with an exceptional physical constitution, as I am cursed with an exceptional mental character, I shall not much longer groan under the wearisome burthen of this earthly existence. If it were to be otherwise – if I were to live on to the age most men desire and provide for – I should for once have known whether the miseries of delusive expectation can outweigh the miseries of true prevision. For I foresee when I shall die, and everything that will happen in my last moments.

Just a month from this day, on the 20th of September 1850, I shall be sitting in this chair, in this study, at ten o'clock at night, longing to die, weary of incessant insight and foresight, without delusions and without hope. Just as I am watching a tongue of blue flame rising in the fire, and my lamp is burning low, the horrible contraction will begin at my chest. I shall only have time to reach the bell, and pull it violently, before the sense of suffocation will come. No one will answer my bell. I know why. My two servants are lovers, and will have quarrelled. My housekeeper will have rushed out of the house in a fury, two hours before, hoping that Perry will believe she has gone to drown herself. Perry is alarmed at last, and is gone out after her. The little scullery-maid is asleep on a bench: she never answers the bell; it does not wake her. The sense of suffocation increases: my lamp goes out with a horrible stench: I make a great effort, and snatch at the bell again. I long for life, and there is no help. I thirsted for the unknown: the thirst is gone. O God, let me stay with the known, and be weary of it: I am content. Agony of pain and suffocation – and all the while the earth, the fields, the pebbly brook at the bottom of the rookery, the fresh scent after the rain, the light of the morning through my chamber-window, the warmth of the hearth after the frosty air – will darkness close over them for ever?

Darkness – darkness – no pain – nothing but darkness: but I am passing on and on through the darkness: my thought stays in the darkness, but always with a sense of moving onward . . .

Before that time comes, I wish to use my last hours of ease and strength in telling the strange story of my experience. I have never fully unbosomed myself to any human being; I have never been encouraged to trust much in the sympathy of my fellow-men. But we have all a chance of meeting with some pity, some tenderness, some charity, when we are dead: it is the living only who cannot be forgiven – the living only from whom men's indulgence and reverence are held off, like the rain by the hard east wind. While the heart beats, bruise it – it is your only opportunity; while the eye can still turn towards you with moist timid entreaty, freeze it with an icy unanswering gaze; while the ear, that delicate messenger to the inmost sanctuary of the soul, can still take in the tones of kindness, put it off with hard civility, or sneering compliment, or envious affectation of indifference; while the creative brain can still throb with the sense of injustice, with the yearning for brotherly recognition – make haste – oppress it with your ill-considered judgments, your trivial comparisons, your careless misrepresentations. The heart will by-and-by be still – *ubi sæva indignatio ulterius cor lacerare nequit;** the eye will cease to entreat; the ear will be deaf; the brain will have ceased from all wants as well as from all work. Then your charitable speeches may find vent; then you may remember and pity the toil and the struggle and the failure; then you may give due honour to the work achieved; then you may find extenuation for errors, and may consent to bury them.

That is a trivial schoolboy text; why do I dwell on it? It has little reference to me, for I shall leave no works behind me for men to honour. I have no near relatives who will make up, by weeping over my grave, for the wounds they

---

*   Inscription on Swift's tombstone.

inflicted on me when I was among them. It is only the story of my life that will perhaps win a little more sympathy from strangers when I am dead, than I ever believed it would obtain from my friends while I was living.

My childhood perhaps seems happier to me than it really was, by contrast with all the after-years. For then the curtain of the future was as impenetrable to me as to other children: I had all their delight in the present hour, their sweet indefinite hopes for the morrow; and I had a tender mother: even now, after the dreary lapse of long years, a slight trace of sensation accompanies the remembrance of her caress as she held me on her knee – her arms round my little body, her cheek pressed on mine. I had a complaint of the eyes that made me blind for a little while, and she kept me on her knee from morning till night. That unequalled love soon vanished out of my life, and even to my childish consciousness it was as if that life had become more chill. I rode my little white pony with the groom by my side as before, but there were no loving eyes looking at me as I mounted, no glad arms opened to me when I came back. Perhaps I missed my mother's love more than most children of seven or eight would have done, to whom the other pleasures of life remained as before; for I was certainly a very sensitive child. I remember still the mingled trepidation and delicious excitement with which I was affected by the tramping of the horses on the pavement in the echoing stables, by the loud resonance of the grooms' voices, by the booming bark of the dogs as my father's carriage thundered under the archway of the courtyard, by the din of the gong as it gave notice of luncheon and dinner. The measured tramp of soldiery which I sometimes heard – for my father's house lay near a county town where there were large barracks – made me sob and tremble; and yet when they were gone past, I longed for them to come back again.

I fancy my father thought me an odd child, and had little fondness for me; though he was very careful in fulfilling what he regarded as a parent's duties. But he was already past the middle of life, and I was not his only son. My mother had been his second wife, and he was five-and-forty when he married her. He was a firm, unbending, intensely orderly man, in root and stem a banker, but with a flourishing graft of the active landholder, aspiring to county influence: one of those people who are always like themselves from day to day, who are uninfluenced by the weather, and neither know melancholy nor high spirits. I held him in great awe, and appeared more timid and sensitive in his presence than at other times; a circumstance which, perhaps, helped to confirm him in the intention to educate me on a different plan from the prescriptive one with which he had complied in the case of my elder brother, already a tall youth at Eton. My brother was to be his representative and successor; he must go to Eton and Oxford, for the sake of making connections, of course: my father was not a man to underrate the bearing of Latin satirists or Greek dramatists on the attainment of an aristocratic position. But, intrinsically, he had slight esteem for 'those dead but sceptred spirits;' having qualified himself for forming an independent opinion by reading Potter's 'Æschylus,' and dipping into Francis's 'Horace.' To this negative view he added a positive one, derived, from a recent connection with mining speculations; namely, that a scientific education was the really useful training for a younger son. Moreover, it was clear that a shy, sensitive boy like me was not fit to encounter the rough experience of a public school. Mr Letherall had said so very decidedly. Mr Letherall was a large man in spectacles, who one day took my small head between his large hands, and pressed it here and there in an exploratory, suspicious manner – then placed each of his great thumbs on my temples, and pushed me a little way from him, and stared at me with glittering spectacles. The contemplation appeared to displease him, for he frowned sternly, and said to my father, drawing his thumbs across my eyebrows –

'The deficiency is there, sir – there; and here,' he added, touching the upper sides of my head, 'here is the excess. That must be brought out, sir, and this must be laid to sleep.'

I was in a state of tremor, partly at the vague idea that I was the object of reprobation, partly in the agitation of my first hatred – hatred of this big, spectacled man, who pulled my head about as if he wanted to buy and cheapen it.

I am not aware how much Mr Letherall had to do with the system afterwards adopted towards me, but it was presently clear that private tutors, natural history, science, and the modern languages, were the appliances by which the defects of my organisation were to be remedied. I was very stupid about machines, so I was to be greatly occupied with them; I had no memory for classification, so it was particularly necessary that I should study systematic zoology and botany; I was hungry for human deeds and human emotions, so I was to be plentifully crammed with the mechanical powers, the elementary bodies, and the phenomena of electricity and magnetism. A better-constituted boy would certainly have profited under my intelligent tutors, with their scientific apparatus; and would, doubtless, have found the phenomena of electricity and magnetism as fascinating as I was, every Thursday, assured they were. As it was, I could have paired off, for ignorance of whatever was taught me, with the worst Latin scholar that was ever turned out of a classical academy. I read Plutarch, and Shakspere, and Don Quixote by the sly, and supplied myself in that way with wandering thoughts, while my tutor was assuring me that 'an improved man, as distinguished from an ignorant one, was a man who knew the reason why water ran down-hill.' I had no desire to be this improved man; I was glad of the running water; I could watch it and listen to it gurgling among the pebbles, and bathing the bright green water-plants, by the hour together. I did not want to know *why* it ran; I had perfect confidence that there were good reasons for what was so very beautiful.

There is no need to dwell on this part of my life. I have said enough to indicate that my nature was of the sensitive, unpractical order, and that it grew up in an uncongenial medium, which could never foster it into happy, healthy development. When I was sixteen I was sent to Geneva to complete my course of education; and the change was a very happy one to me, for the first sight of the Alps, with the setting sun on them, as we descended the Jura, seemed to me like an entrance into heaven; and the three years of my life there were spent in a perpetual sense of exaltation, as if from a draught of delicious wine, at the presence of Nature in all her awful loveliness. You will think, perhaps, that I must have been a poet, from this early sensibility to Nature. But my lot was not so happy as that. A poet pours forth his song and *believes* in the listening ear and answering soul, to which his song will be floated sooner or later. But the poet's sensibility without his voice – the poet's sensibility that finds no vent but in silent tears on the sunny bank, when the noonday light sparkles on the water, or in an inward shudder at the sound of harsh human tones, the sight of a cold human eye – this dumb passion brings with it a fatal solitude of soul in the society of one's fellow-men. My least solitary moments were those in which I pushed off in my boat, at evening, towards the centre of the lake; it seemed to me that the sky, and the glowing mountain-tops, and the wide blue water, surrounded me with a cherishing love such as no human face had shed on me since my mother's love had vanished out of my life. I used to do as Jean Jacques did – lie down in my boat and let it glide where it would, while I looked up at the departing glow leaving one mountain-top after the other, as if the prophet's chariot of fire were passing over them on its way to the home of light. Then, when the white summits were all sad and corpse-like, I had to push homeward, for I was under careful surveillance, and was allowed no late wanderings. This disposition of mine was not favourable to the formation of intimate friendships among the numerous youths of my own age who are always to be found studying at Geneva. Yet I made *one* such friendship; and, singularly enough, it was with a youth whose intellectual tendencies were the very reverse of my own. I shall call him Charles Meunier; his real surname – an English one, for he was of English extraction – having since become celebrated. He was an orphan, who lived on a miserable pittance while he pursued the medical studies for which he had a special genius. Strange! that with my vague mind, susceptible and unobservant, hating inquiry and given up to contemplation, I should have been drawn towards a youth whose strongest passion was science. But the bond was not an intellectual one; it came from a source that can happily blend the stupid with the brilliant, the dreamy with the practical: it came from community of feeling.

Charles was poor and ugly, derided by Genevese *gamins*, and not acceptable in drawing-rooms. I saw that he was isolated, as I was, though from a different cause, and, stimulated by a sympathetic resentment, I made timid advances towards him. It is enough to say that there sprang up as much comradeship between us as our different habits would allow; and in Charles's rare holidays we went up the Salève together, or took the boat to Vevay, while I listened dreamily to the monologues in which he unfolded his bold conceptions of future experiment and discovery. I mingled them confusedly in my thought with glimpses of blue water and delicate floating cloud, with the notes of birds and the distant glitter of the glacier. He knew quite well that my mind was half absent, yet he liked to talk to me in this way; for don't we talk of our hopes and our projects even to dogs and birds, when they love us? I have mentioned this one friendship because of its connection with a strange and terrible scene which I shall have to narrate in my subsequent life.

This happier life at Geneva was put an end to by a severe illness, which is partly a blank to me, partly a time of dimly-remembered suffering, with the presence of my father by my bed from time to time. Then came the languid monotony of convalescence, the days gradually breaking into variety and distinctness as my strength enabled me to take longer and longer drives. On one of these more vividly remembered days, my father said to me, as he sat beside my sofa –

'When you are quite well enough to travel, Latimer, I shall take you home with me. The journey will amuse you and do you good, for I shall go through the Tyrol and Austria, and you will see many new places. Our neighbours, the Filmores, are come; Alfred will join us at Basle, and we shall all go together to Vienna, and back by Prague' . . .

My father was called away before he had finished his sentence, and he left my mind resting on the word *Prague*, with a strange sense that a new and wondrous scene was breaking upon me: a city under the broad sunshine, that seemed to me as if it were the summer sunshine of a long-past century arrested in its course – unrefreshed for ages by the dews of night, or the rushing rain-cloud; scorching the dusty, weary, time-eaten grandeur of a people doomed to live on in the stale repetition of memories, like deposed and superannuated kings in their regal gold-inwoven tatters. The city looked so thirsty that the broad river seemed to me a sheet of metal; and the blackened statues, as I passed under their blank gaze, along the unending bridge, with their ancient garments and their saintly crowns, seemed to me the real inhabitants and owners of this place, while the busy, trivial men and women, hurrying to and fro, were a swarm of ephemeral visitants infesting it for a day. It is such grim, stony beings as these, I thought, who are the fathers of ancient faded children, in those tanned time-fretted dwellings that crowd the steep before me; who pay their court in the worn and crumbling pomp of the palace which stretches its monotonous length on the height; who worship wearily in the stifling air of the churches, urged by no fear or hope, but compelled by their doom to be ever old and undying, to live on in the rigidity of habit, as they live on in perpetual mid-day, without the repose of night or the new birth of morning.

A stunning clang of metal suddenly thrilled through me, and I became conscious of the objects in my room again: one of the fire-irons had fallen as Pierre opened the door to bring me my draught. My heart was palpitating violently, and I begged Pierre to leave my draught beside me; I would take it presently.

As soon as I was alone again, I began to ask myself whether I had been sleeping. Was this a dream – this wonderfully distinct vision – minute in its distinctness down to a patch of rainbow light on the pavement, transmitted through a coloured lamp in the shape of a star – of a strange city, quite unfamiliar to my imagination? I had seen no picture of Prague: it lay in my mind as a mere name, with vaguely-remembered historical associations – ill-defined memories of imperial grandeur and religious wars.

Nothing of this sort had ever occurred in my dreaming experience before, for I had often been humiliated because my dreams were only saved from being utterly disjointed and commonplace by the frequent terrors of nightmare. But I could not believe that I had been asleep, for I remembered distinctly the gradual breaking-in of the vision upon me, like the new images in a dissolving view, or the growing distinctness of the landscape as the sun lifts up the veil of the morning mist. And while I was conscious of this incipient vision, I was also conscious that Pierre came to tell my father Mr Filmore was waiting for him, and that my father hurried out of the room. No, it was not a dream; was it – the thought was full of tremulous exultation – was it the poet's nature in me, hitherto only a troubled yearning sensibility, now manifesting itself suddenly as spontaneous creation? Surely it was in this way that Homer saw the plain of Troy, that Dante saw the abodes of the departed, that Milton saw the earthward flight of the Tempter. Was it that my illness had wrought some happy change in my organisation – given a firmer tension to my nerves – carried off some dull obstruction? I had often read of such effects – in works of fiction at least. Nay; in genuine biographies I had read of the subtilising or exalting influence of some diseases on the mental powers. Did not Novalis feel his inspiration intensified under the progress of consumption?

When my mind had dwelt for some time on this blissful idea, it seemed to me that I might perhaps test it by an exertion of my will. The vision had begun when my father was speaking of our going to Prague. I did not for a moment believe it was really a representation of that city; I believed – I hoped it was a picture that my newly-liberated genius had painted in fiery haste, with the colours snatched from lazy memory. Suppose I were to fix my mind on some other place – Venice, for example, which was far more familiar to my imagination than Prague: perhaps the same sort of result would follow. I concentrated my thoughts on Venice; I stimulated my imagination with poetic memories, and strove to feel myself present in Venice, as I had felt myself present in Prague. But in vain. I was only colouring the Canaletto engravings that hung in my old bedroom at home; the picture was a shifting one, my mind wandering uncertainly in search of more vivid images; I could see no accident of form or shadow without conscious labour after the necessary conditions. It was all prosaic effort, not rapt passivity, such as I had experienced half an hour before. I was discouraged; but I remembered that inspiration was fitful.

For several days I was in a state of excited expectation, watching for a recurrence of my new gift. I sent my thoughts ranging over my world of knowledge, in the hope that they would find some object which would send a reawakening vibration through my slumbering genius. But no; my world remained as dim as ever, and that flash of strange light refused to come again, though I watched for it with palpitating eagerness.

My father accompanied me every day in a drive, and a gradually lengthening walk as my powers of walking increased; and one evening he had agreed to come and fetch me at twelve the next day, that we might go together to select a musical box, and other purchases rigorously demanded of a rich Englishman visiting Geneva. He was one of the most punctual of men and bankers, and I was always nervously anxious to be quite ready for him at the appointed time. But, to my surprise, at a quarter past twelve he had not appeared. I felt all the impatience of a convalescent who has nothing particular to do, and who has just taken a tonic in the prospect of immediate exercise that would carry off the stimulus.

Unable to sit still and reserve my strength, I walked up and down the room, looking out on the current of the Rhone, just where it leaves the dark-blue lake; but thinking all the while of the possible causes that could detain my father.

Suddenly I was conscious that my father was in the room, but not alone: there were two persons with him. Strange! I had heard no footstep, I had not seen the door open; but I saw my father, and at his right hand our neighbour Mrs Filmore, whom I remembered very well, though I had not seen her for five years. She was a commonplace middle-aged woman, in silk and cashmere; but the lady on the left of my father was not more than twenty, a tall, slim, willowy figure, with luxuriant blond hair, arranged in cunning braids and folds that looked almost too massive for the slight figure and the small-featured, thin-lipped face they crowned. But the face had not a girlish expression: the features were sharp, the pale grey eyes at once acute, restless, and sarcastic. They were fixed on me in half-smiling curiosity, and I felt a painful sensation as if a sharp wind were cutting me. The pale green dress, and the green leaves that seemed to form a border about her pale blond hair, made me think of a Water-Nixie, – for my mind was full of German lyrics, and this pale, fatal-eyed woman, with the green weeds, looked like a birth from some cold sedgy stream, the daughter of an aged river.

'Well, Latimer, you thought me long,' my father said . . .

But while the last word was in my ears, the whole group vanished, and there was nothing between me and the Chinese painted folding-screen that stood before the door. I was cold and trembling; I could only totter forward and throw myself on the sofa. This strange new power had manifested itself again . . . But *was* it a power? Might it not rather be a disease – a sort of intermittent delirium, concentrating my energy of brain into moments of unhealthy activity, and leaving my saner hours all the more barren? I felt a dizzy sense of unreality in what my eye rested on; I grasped the bell convulsively, like one trying to free himself from nightmare, and rang it twice. Pierre came with a look of alarm in his face.

'Monsieur ne se trouve pas bien?' he said, anxiously.

'I'm tired of waiting, Pierre,' I said, as distinctly and emphatically as I could, like a man determined to be sober in spite of wine; 'I'm afraid something has happened to my father – he's usually so punctual. Run to the Hôtel des Bergues and see if he is there.'

Pierre left the room at once, with a soothing 'Bien, Monsieur;' and I felt the better for this scene of simple, waking prose. Seeking to calm myself still further, I went into my bedroom, adjoining the *salon*, and opened a case of eau-de-Cologne; took out a bottle; went through the process of taking out the cork very neatly, and then rubbed the reviving spirit over my hands and forehead, and under my nostrils, drawing a new delight from the scent because I had procured it by slow details of labour, and by no strange sudden madness. Already I had begun to taste something of the horror that belongs to the lot of a human being whose nature is not adjusted to simple human conditions.

Still enjoying the scent, I returned to the *salon*, but it was not unoccupied, as it had been before I left it. In front of the Chinese folding-screen there was my father, with Mrs Filmore on his right hand, and on his left—the slim blond-haired girl, with the keen face and the keen eyes fixed on me in half-smiling curiosity.

'Well, Latimer, you thought me long,' my father said . . .

I heard no more, felt no more, till I became conscious that I was lying with my head low on the sofa, Pierre and my father by my side. As soon as I was thoroughly revived, my father left the room, and presently returned, saying –

'I've been to tell the ladies how you are, Latimer. They were waiting in the next room. We shall put off our shopping expedition to-day.'

Presently he said, 'That young lady is Bertha Grant, Mrs Filmore's orphan niece. Filmore has adopted her, and she lives with them, so you will have her for a neighbour when we go home – perhaps for a near relation; for there is a tenderness between her and Alfred, I suspect, and I should be gratified by the match, since Filmore means to provide for her in every way as if she were his daughter. It had not occurred to me that you knew nothing about her living with the Filmores.'

He made no further allusion to the fact of my having fainted at the moment of seeing her, and I would not for the world have told him the reason: I shrank from the idea of disclosing to any one what might be regarded as a pitiable peculiarity, most of all from betraying it to my father, who would have suspected my sanity ever after.

I do not mean to dwell with particularity on the details of my experience. I have described these two cases at length, because they had definite, clearly traceable results in my after-lot.

Shortly after this last occurrence – I think the very next day – I began to be aware of a phase in my abnormal sensibility, to which, from the languid and slight nature of my intercourse with others since my illness, I had not been alive before. This was the obtrusion on my mind of the mental process going forward in first one person, and then another, with whom I happened to be in contact: the vagrant, frivolous ideas and emotions of some uninteresting acquaintance – Mrs Filmore, for example – would force themselves on my consciousness like an importunate, ill-played musical instrument, or the loud activity of an imprisoned insect. But this unpleasant sensibility was fitful, and left me moments of rest, when the souls of my companions were once more shut out from me, and I felt a relief such as silence brings to wearied nerves. I might have believed this importunate insight to be merely a diseased activity of the imagination, but that my prevision of incalculable words and actions proved it to have a fixed relation to the mental process in other minds. But this superadded consciousness, wearying and annoying enough when it urged on me the trivial experience of indifferent people, became an intense pain and grief when it seemed to be opening to me the souls of those who were in a close relation to me – when the rational talk, the graceful attentions, the wittily-turned phrases, and the kindly deeds, which used to make the web of their characters, were seen as if thrust asunder by a microscopic vision, that showed all the intermediate frivolities, all the suppressed egoism, all the struggling chaos of puerilities, meanness, vague capricious memories, and indolent make-shift thoughts, from which human words and deeds emerge like leaflets covering a fermenting heap.

At Basle we were joined by my brother Alfred, now a handsome self-confident man of six-and-twenty – a thorough contrast to my fragile, nervous, ineffectual self. I believe I was held to have a sort of half-womanish, half-ghostly beauty; for the portrait-painters, who are thick as weeds at Geneva, had often asked me to sit to them, and I had been the model of a dying minstrel in a fancy picture. But I thoroughly disliked my own *physique*, and nothing but the belief that it was a condition of poetic genius would have reconciled me to it. That brief hope was quite fled, and I saw in my face now nothing but the stamp of a morbid organisation, framed for passive suffering – too feeble for the sublime resistance of poetic production. Alfred, from whom I had been almost constantly separated, and who, in his present stage of character and appearance, came before me as a perfect stranger, was bent on being extremely friendly and brother-like to me. He had the superficial kindness of a good-humoured, self-satisfied nature, that fears no rivalry, and has encountered no contrarieties. I am not sure that my disposition was good enough for me to have been quite free from envy towards him, even if our desires had not clashed, and if I had been in the healthy human condition which admits of generous confidence and charitable construction. There must always have been an antipathy between our natures. As it was, he became in a few weeks an object of intense hatred to me; and when he entered the room, still more when he spoke, it was as if a sensation of grating metal had set my teeth on edge. My diseased consciousness was more intensely and continually occupied with his thoughts and emotions, than with those of any other person who came in my way. I was perpetually exasperated with the petty promptings of his conceit and his love of patronage, with his self-complacent belief in Bertha Grant's passion for him, with his half-pitying contempt for me – seen not in the ordinary indications of intonation and phrase and slight action, which an acute and suspicious mind is on the watch for, but in all their naked skinless complication.

For we were rivals, and our desires clashed, though he was not aware of it. I have said nothing yet of the effect Bertha Grant produced in me on a nearer acquaintance. That effect was chiefly determined by the fact that she made the only exception, among all the human beings about me, to my unhappy gift of insight. About Bertha I was always in a state of uncertainty: I could watch the expression of her face, and speculate on its meaning; I could ask for her opinion with the real interest of ignorance; I could listen for her words and watch for her smile with hope and fear: she had for me the fascination of an unravelled destiny. I say it was this fact that chiefly determined the strong effect she produced on me: for, in the abstract, no womanly character could seem to have less affinity for that of a shrinking, romantic, passionate youth than Bertha's. She was keen, sarcastic, unimaginative, prematurely cynical, remaining critical and unmoved in the most impressive scenes, inclined to dissect all my favourite poems, and especially contemptuous towards the German lyrics which were my pet literature at that time. To this moment I am unable to define my feeling towards her: it was not ordinary boyish admiration, for she was the very opposite, even to the colour of her hair, of the ideal woman who still remained to me the type of loveliness; and she was without that enthusiasm for the great and good, which, even at the moment of her strongest dominion over me, I should have declared to be the highest element of character. But there is no tyranny more complete than that which a self-centred negative nature exercises over a morbidly sensitive nature perpetually craving sympathy and support. The most independent people feel the effect of a man's silence in heightening their value for his opinion – feel an additional triumph in conquering the reverence of a critic habitually captious and satirical: no wonder, then, that an enthusiastic self-distrusting youth should watch and wait before the closed secret of a sarcastic woman's face, as if it were the shrine of the doubtfully benignant deity who ruled his destiny. For a young enthusiast is unable to imagine the total negation in another mind of the emotions which are stirring his own: they may be feeble, latent, inactive, he thinks, but they are there – they may be called forth; sometimes, in moments of happy hallucination, he believes they may be there in all the greater strength because he sees no outward sign of them. And this effect, as I have intimated, was heightened to its utmost intensity in me, because Bertha was the only being who remained for me in the mysterious seclusion of soul that renders such youthful delusion possible. Doubtless there was another sort of fascination at work – that subtle physical attraction which delights in cheating our psychological predictions, and in compelling the men who paint sylphs, to fall in love with some *bonne et brave femme*, heavy-heeled and freckled.

Bertha's behaviour towards me was such as to encourage all my illusions, to heighten my boyish passion, and make me more and more dependent on her smiles. Looking back with my present wretched knowledge, I conclude that her vanity and love of power were intensely gratified by the belief that I had fainted on first seeing her purely from the strong impression her person had produced on me. The most prosaic woman likes to believe herself the object of a violent, a poetic passion; and without a grain of romance in her, Bertha had that spirit of intrigue which gave piquancy to the idea that the brother of the man she meant to marry was dying with love and jealousy for her sake. That she meant to marry my brother, was what at that time I did not believe; for though he was assiduous in his attentions to her, and I knew well enough that both he and my father had made up their minds to this result, there was not yet an understood engagement – there had been no explicit declaration; and Bertha habitually, while she flirted with my brother, and accepted his homage in a way that implied to him a thorough recognition of its intention, made me believe, by the subtlest looks and phrases – feminine nothings which could never be quoted against her – that he was really the object of her secret ridicule; that she thought him, as I did, a cox-comb, whom she would have pleasure in disappointing. Me she openly petted in my brother's presence, as if I were too young and sickly ever to be thought of as a lover; and that was the view he took of me. But I believe she must inwardly have delighted in the tremors into which she threw me by the coaxing way in which she patted my curls, while she laughed at my quotations. Such caresses were always given in the presence of our friends; for when we were alone together, she affected a much greater dis-tance towards me, and now and then took the opportunity, by words or slight actions, to stimulate my foolish timid hope that she really preferred me. And why should she not follow her inclination? I was not in so advantageous a position as my brother, but I had fortune, I was not a year younger than she was, and she was an heiress, who would soon be of age to decide for herself.

The fluctuations of hope and fear, confined to this one channel, made each day in her presence a delicious torment. There was one deliberate act of hers which espe-cially helped to intoxicate me. When we were at Vienna her twentieth birthday occurred, and as she was very fond of ornaments, we all took the opportunity of the splendid jewellers' shops in that Teutonic Paris to purchase her a birthday present of jewellery. Mine, naturally, was the least expensive; it was an opal ring – the opal was my favourite stone, because it seems to blush and turn pale as if it had a soul. I told Bertha so when I gave it her, and said that it was an emblem of the poetic nature, changing with the changing light of heaven and of woman's eyes. In the evening she appeared elegantly dressed, and wearing conspicuously all the birthday presents except mine. I looked eagerly at her fingers, but saw no opal. I had no opportunity of noticing this to her during the evening; but the next day, when I found her seated near the window alone, after breakfast, I said, 'You scorn to wear my poor opal. I should have remembered that you despised poetic natures, and should have given you coral, or turquoise, or some other opaque unresponsive stone.' 'Do I despise it?' she answered, taking hold of a delicate gold chain which she always wore round her neck and drawing out the end from her bosom with my ring hanging to it; 'it hurts me a little, I can tell you,' she said, with her usual dubious smile, 'to wear it in that secret place; and since your poetical nature is so stupid as to prefer a more public position, I shall not endure the pain any longer.'

She took off the ring from the chain and put it on her finger, smiling still, while the blood rushed to my cheeks, and I could not trust myself to say a word of entreaty that she would keep the ring where it was before.

I was completely fooled by this, and for two days shut myself up in my own room whenever Bertha was absent, that I might intoxicate myself afresh with the thought of this scene and all it implied.

I should mention that during these two months – which seemed a long life to me from the novelty and intensity of the pleasures and pains I underwent – my diseased participation in other people's consciousness continued to torment me; now it was my father, and now my brother, now Mrs Filmore or her husband, and now our German courier, whose stream of thought rushed upon me like a ringing in the ears not to be got rid of, though it allowed my own impulses and ideas to continue their uninterrupted course. It was like a preternaturally heightened sense of hearing, making audible to one a roar of sound where others find perfect stillness. The weariness and disgust of this involuntary intrusion into other souls was counteracted only by my ignorance of Bertha, and my growing passion for her; a passion enormously stimulated, if not produced, by that ignorance. She was my oasis of mystery in the dreary desert of knowledge. I had never allowed my diseased condition to betray itself, or to drive me into any unusual speech or action, except once, when, in a moment of peculiar bitterness against my brother, I had forestalled some words which I knew he was going to utter – a clever observation, which he had prepared beforehand. He had occasionally a slightly-affected hesitation in his speech, and when he paused an instant after the second word, my impatience and jealousy impelled me to continue the speech for him, as if it were something we had both learned by rote. He coloured and looked astonished, as well as annoyed; and the words had no sooner escaped my lips than I felt a shock of alarm lest such an anticipation of words – very far from being words of course, easy to divine – should have betrayed me as an exceptional being, a sort of quiet energumen, whom every one, Bertha above all, would shudder at and avoid. But I magnified, as usual, the impression any word or deed of mine could produce on others; for no one gave any sign of having noticed my interruption as more than a rudeness, to be forgiven me on the score of my feeble nervous condition.

While this superadded consciousness of the actual was almost constant with me, I had never had a recurrence of that distinct prevision which I have described in relation to my first interview with Bertha; and I was waiting with eager curiosity to know whether or not my vision of Prague would prove to have been an instance of the same kind. A few days after the incident of the opal ring, we were paying one of our frequent visits to the Lichtenberg Palace. I could never look at many pictures in succession; for pictures, when they are at all powerful, affect me so strongly that one or two exhaust all my capability of contemplation. This morning I had been looking at Giorgione's picture of the cruel-eyed woman, said to be a likeness of Lucrezia Borgia. I had stood long alone before it, fascinated by the terrible reality of that cunning, relentless face, till I felt a strange poisoned sensation, as if I had long been inhaling a fatal odour, and was just beginning to be conscious of its effects. Perhaps even then I should not have moved away, if the rest of the party had not returned to this room, and announced that they were going to the Belvedere Gallery to settle a bet which had arisen between my brother and Mr Filmore about a portrait. I followed them dreamily, and was hardly alive to what occurred till they had all gone up to the gallery, leaving me below; for I refused to come within sight of another picture that day. I made my way to the Grand Terrace, since it was agreed that we should saunter in the gardens when the dispute had been decided. I had been sitting here a short space, vaguely conscious of trim gardens, with a city and green hills in the distance, when, wishing to avoid the proximity of the sentinel, I rose and walked down the broad stone steps, intending to seat myself farther on in the gardens. Just as I reached the gravel-walk, I felt an arm slipped within mine, and a light hand gently pressing my wrist. In the same instant a strange intoxicating numbness passed over me, like the continuance or climax of the sensation I was still feeling from the gaze of Lucrezia Borgia. The gardens, the summer sky, the consciousness of Bertha's arm being within mine, all vanished, and I seemed to be suddenly in darkness, out of which there gradually broke a dim firelight, and I felt myself sitting in my father's leather chair in the library at home. I knew the fireplace – the dogs for the wood-fire – the black marble chimney-piece with the white marble medallion of the dying Cleopatra in the centre. Intense and hopeless misery was pressing on my soul; the light became stronger, for Bertha was entering with a candle in her hand – Bertha, my wife – with cruel eyes, with green jewels and green leaves on her white ball-dress; every hateful thought within her present to me . . . 'Madman, idiot! why don't you kill yourself, then?' It was a moment of hell. I saw into her pitiless soul – saw its barren worldliness, its scorching hate – and felt it clothe me round like an air I was obliged to breathe. She came with her candle and stood over me with a bitter smile of contempt; I saw the great emerald brooch on her bosom, a studded serpent with diamond eyes. I shuddered – I despised this woman with the barren soul and mean thoughts; but I felt helpless before her, as if she clutched my bleeding heart, and would clutch it till the last drop of life-blood ebbed away. She was my wife, and we hated each other. Gradually the hearth, the dim library, the candle-light disappeared – seemed to melt away into a background of light, the green serpent with the diamond eyes remaining a dark image on the retina. Then I had a sense of my eyelids quivering, and the living daylight broke in upon me; I saw gardens, and heard voices; I was seated on the steps of the Belvedere Terrace, and my friends were round me.

The tumult of mind into which I was thrown by this hideous vision made me ill for several days, and pro-longed our stay at Vienna. I shuddered with horror as the scene recurred to me; and it recurred constantly, with all its minutiæ, as if they had been burnt into my mem-ory; and yet, such is the madness of the human heart

33

under the influence of its immediate desires, I felt a wild hell-braving joy that Bertha was to be mine; for the fulfilment of my former prevision concerning her first appearance before me, left me little hope that this last hideous glimpse of the future was the mere diseased play of my own mind, and had no relation to external realities. One thing alone I looked towards as a possible means of casting doubt on my terrible conviction – the discovery that my vision of Prague had been false – and Prague was the next city on our route.

Meanwhile, I was no sooner in Bertha's society again, than I was as completely under her sway as before. What if I saw into the heart of Bertha, the matured woman – Bertha, my wife? Bertha, the *girl*, was a fascinating secret to me still: I trembled under her touch; I felt the witchery of her presence; I yearned to be assured of her love. The fear of poison is feeble against the sense of thirst. Nay, I was just as jealous of my brother as before – just as much irritated by his small patronising ways; for my pride, my diseased sensibility, were there as they had always been, and winced as inevitably under every offence as my eye winced from an intruding mote. The future, even when brought within the compass of feeling by a vision that made me shudder, had still no more than the force of an idea, compared with the force of present emotion – of my love for Bertha, of my dislike and jealousy towards my brother.

It is an old story, that men sell themselves to the

tempter, and sign a bond with their blood, because it is only to take effect at a distant day; then rush on to snatch the cup their souls thirst after with an impulse not the less savage because there is a dark shadow beside them for evermore. There is no short cut, no patent tram-road, to wisdom: after all the centuries of invention, the soul's path lies through the thorny wilderness which must be still trodden in solitude, with bleeding feet, with sobs for help, as it was trodden by them of old time.

My mind speculated eagerly on the means by which I should become my brother's successful rival, for I was still too timid, in my ignorance of Bertha's actual feeling, to venture on any step that would urge from her an avowal of it. I thought I should gain confidence even for this, if my vision of Prague proved to have been veracious; and yet, the horror of that certitude! Behind the slim girl Bertha, whose words and looks I watched for, whose touch was bliss, there stood continually that Bertha with the fuller form, the harder eyes, the more rigid mouth, – with the barren selfish soul laid bare; no longer a fascinating secret, but a measured fact, urging itself perpetually on my unwilling sight. Are you unable to give me your sympathy – you who read this? Are you unable to imagine this double consciousness at work within me, flowing on like two parallel streams which never mingle their waters and blend into a common hue? Yet you must have known something of the presentiments that spring from an insight at war with passion;

and my visions were only like presentiments intensified to horror. You have known the powerlessness of ideas before the might of impulse; and my visions, when once they had passed into memory, were mere ideas – pale shadows that beckoned in vain, while my hand was grasped by the living and the loved.

In after-days I thought with bitter regret that if I had foreseen something more or something different – if instead of that hideous vision which poisoned the passion it could not destroy, or if even along with it I could have had a foreshadowing of that moment when I looked on my brother's face for the last time, some softening influence would have been shed over my feeling towards him: pride and hatred would surely have been subdued into pity, and the record of those hidden sins would have been shortened. But this is one of the vain thoughts with which we men flatter ourselves. We try to believe that the egoism within us would have easily been melted, and that it was only the narrowness of our knowledge which hemmed in our generosity, our awe, our human piety, and hindered them from submerging our hard indifference to the sensations and emotions of our fellow. Our tenderness and self-renunciation seem strong when our egoism has had its day – when, after our mean striving for a triumph that is to be another's loss, the triumph comes suddenly, and we shudder at it, because it is held out by the chill hand of death.

Our arrival in Prague happened at night, and I was

glad of this, for it seemed like a deferring of a terribly decisive moment, to be in the city for hours without seeing it. As we were not to remain long in Prague, but to go on speedily to Dresden, it was proposed that we should drive out the next morning and take a general view of the place, as well as visit some of its specially interesting spots, before the heat became oppressive – for we were in August, and the season was hot and dry. But it happened that the ladies were rather late at their morning toilet, and to my father's politely-repressed but perceptible annoyance, we were not in the carriage till the morning was far advanced. I thought with a sense of relief, as we entered the Jews' quarter, where we were to visit the old synagogue, that we should be kept in this flat, shut-up part of the city, until we should all be too tired and too warm to go farther, and so we should return without seeing more than the streets through which we had already passed. That would give me another day's suspense – suspense, the only form in which a fearful spirit knows the solace of hope. But, as I stood under the blackened, groined arches of that old synagogue, made dimly visible by the seven thin candles in the sacred lamp, while our Jewish cicerone reached down the Book of the Law, and read to us in its ancient tongue, – I felt a shuddering impression that this strange building, with its shrunken lights, this surviving withered remnant of medieval Judaism, was of a piece with my vision. Those darkened dusty Christian saints, with their loftier arches and their larger candles, needed the consolatory scorn with which they might point to a more shrivelled death-in-life than their own.

As I expected, when we left the Jews' quarter the elders of our party wished to return to the hotel. But now, instead of rejoicing in this, as I had done beforehand, I felt a sudden overpowering impulse to go on at once to the bridge, and put an end to the suspense I had been wishing to protract. I declared, with unusual decision, that I would get out of the carriage and walk on alone; they might return without me. My father, thinking this merely a sample of my usual 'poetic nonsense,' objected that I should only do myself harm by walking in the heat; but when I persisted, he said angrily that I might follow my own absurd devices, but that Schmidt (our courier) must go with me. I assented to this, and set off with Schmidt towards the bridge. I had no sooner passed from under the archway of the grand old gate leading on to the bridge, than a trembling seized me, and I turned cold under the mid-day sun; yet I went on; I was in search of something – a small detail which I remembered with special intensity as part of my vision. There it was – the patch of rainbow light on the pavement transmitted through a lamp in the shape of a star.

Chapter 2

Before the autumn was at an end, and while the brown leaves still stood thick on the beeches in our park, my brother and Bertha were engaged to each other, and it was understood that their marriage was to take place early in the next spring. In spite of the certainty I had felt from that moment on the bridge at Prague, that Bertha would one day be my wife, my constitutional timidity and distrust had continued to benumb me, and the words in which I had sometimes premeditated a confession of my love, had died away unuttered. The same conflict had gone on within me as before – the longing for an assurance of love from Bertha's lips, the dread lest a word of contempt and denial should fall upon me like a corrosive acid. What was the conviction of a distant necessity to me? I trembled under a present glance, I hungered after a present joy, I was clogged and chilled by a present fear. And so the days passed on: I witnessed Bertha's engagement and heard her marriage discussed as if I were under a conscious nightmare – knowing it was a dream that would vanish, but feeling stifled under the grasp of hard-clutching fingers.

When I was not in Bertha's presence – and I was with her very often, for she continued to treat me with a playful patronage that wakened no jealousy in my brother – I spent my time chiefly in wandering, in strolling, or taking long rides while the daylight lasted, and then shutting myself up with my unread books; for books had lost the power of chaining my attention. My self-consciousness was heightened to that pitch of intensity in which our own emotions take the form of a drama which urges itself imperatively on our contemplation, and we begin to weep, less under the sense of our suffering than at the thought of it. I felt a sort of pitying anguish over the pathos of my own lot: the lot of a being finely organised for pain, but with hardly any fibres that responded to pleasure – to whom the idea of future evil robbed the present of its joy, and for whom the idea of future good did not still the uneasiness of a present yearning or a present dread. I went dumbly through that stage of the poet's suffering, in which he feels the delicious pang of utterance, and makes an image of his sorrows.

I was left entirely without remonstrance concerning this dreamy wayward life: I knew my father's thought about me: 'That lad will never be good for anything in life: he may waste his years in an insignificant way on the income that falls to him: I shall not trouble myself about a career for him.'

One mild morning in the beginning of November, it happened that I was standing outside the portico patting lazy old Cæsar, a Newfoundland almost blind with age, the only dog that ever took any notice of me – for the very dogs shunned me, and fawned on the happier people about me – when the groom brought up my brother's horse which was to carry him to the hunt, and my brother himself appeared at the door, florid, broad-chested, and self-complacent, feeling what a good-natured fellow he was not to behave insolently to us all on the strength of his great advantages.

'Latimer, old boy,' he said to me in a tone of compassionate cordiality, 'what a pity it is you don't have a run with the hounds now and then! The finest thing in the world for low spirits!'

'Low spirits!' I thought bitterly, as he rode away; 'that is the sort of phrase with which coarse, narrow natures like yours think to describe experience of which you can know no more than your horse knows. It is to such as you that the good of this world falls: ready dulness, healthy selfishness, good-tempered conceit – these are the keys to happiness.'

The quick thought came, that my selfishness was even stronger than his – it was only a suffering selfishness instead of an enjoying one. But then, again, my exasperating insight into Alfred's self-complacent soul, his freedom from all the doubts and fears, the unsatisfied yearnings, the exquisite tortures of sensitiveness, that had made the web of my life, seemed to absolve me from all bonds towards him. This man needed no pity, no love; those fine influences would have been as little felt by him as the delicate white mist is felt by the rock it caresses. There was no evil in store for *him*: if he was not to marry Bertha, it would be because he had found a lot pleasanter to himself.

Mr Filmore's house lay not more than half a mile beyond our own gates, and whenever I knew my brother was gone in another direction, I went there for the chance of finding Bertha at home. Later on in the day I walked thither. By a rare accident she was alone, and we walked out in the grounds together, for she seldom went on foot beyond the trimly-swept gravel-walks. I remember what a beautiful sylph she looked to me as the low November sun shone on her blond hair, and she tripped along teasing me with her usual light banter, to which I listened half fondly, half moodily; it was all the sign Bertha's mysterious inner self ever made to me. To-day perhaps the moodiness predominated, for I had not yet shaken off the access of jealous hate which my brother had raised in me by his parting patronage. Suddenly I interrupted and startled her by saying, almost fiercely, 'Bertha, how can you love Alfred?'

She looked at me with surprise for a moment, but soon her light smile came again, and she answered sarcastically, 'Why do you suppose I love him?'

'How can you ask that, Bertha?'

'What! your wisdom thinks I must love the man I'm going to marry? The most unpleasant thing in the world. I should quarrel with him; I should be jealous of him;

our *ménage* would be conducted in a very ill-bred manner. A little quiet contempt contributes greatly to the elegance of life.'

'Bertha, that is not your real feeling. Why do you delight in trying to deceive me by inventing such cynical speeches?'

'I need never take the trouble of invention in order to deceive you, my small Tasso' – (that was the mocking name she usually gave me). 'The easiest way to deceive a poet is to tell him the truth.'

She was testing the validity of her epigram in a daring way, and for a moment the shadow of my vision – the Bertha whose soul was no secret to me – passed between me and the radiant girl, the playful sylph whose feelings were a fascinating mystery. I suppose I must have shuddered, or betrayed in some other way my momentary chill of horror.

'Tasso !' she said, seizing my wrist, and peeping round into my face, 'are you really beginning to discern what a heartless girl I am? Why, you are not half the poet I thought you were; you are actually capable of believing the truth about me.'

The shadow passed from between us, and was no longer the object nearest to me. The girl whose light fingers grasped me, whose elfish charming face looked into mine – who, I thought, was betraying an interest in my feelings that she would not have directly avowed, – this warm-breathing presence again possessed my senses and

imagination like a returning syren melody which had
been overpowered for an instant by the roar of threaten-
ing waves. It was a moment as delicious to me as the
waking up to a consciousness of youth after a dream of
middle age. I forgot everything but my passion, and said
with swimming eyes –

'Bertha, shall you love me when we are first married? I
wouldn't mind if you really loved me only for a little while.'

Her look of astonishment, as she loosed my hand and
started away from me recalled me to a sense of my
strange, my criminal indiscretion.

'Forgive me,' I said, hurriedly, as soon as I could speak
again; 'I did not know what I was saying.'

'Ah, Tasso's mad fit has come on, I see,' she answered
quietly, for she had recovered herself sooner than I had.
'Let him go home and keep his head cool. I must go in,
for the sun is setting.'

I left her – full of indignation against myself. I had let
slip words which, if she reflected on them, might rouse
in her a suspicion of my abnormal mental condition – a
suspicion which of all things I dreaded. And besides that,
I was ashamed of the apparent baseness I had committed
in uttering them to my brother's betrothed wife. I wan-
dered home slowly, entering our park through a private
gate instead of by the lodges. As I approached the house,
I saw a man dashing off at full speed from the stable-yard
across the park. Had any accident happened at home?
No; perhaps it was only one of my father's peremptory

business errands that required this headlong haste. Nevertheless I quickened my pace without any distinct motive, and was soon at the house. I will not dwell on the scene I found there. My brother was dead – had been pitched from his horse, and killed on the spot by a concussion of the brain.

I went up to the room where he lay, and where my father was seated beside him with a look of rigid despair. I had shunned my father more than any one since our return home, for the radical antipathy between our natures made my insight into his inner self a constant affliction to me. But now, as I went up to him, and stood beside him in sad silence, I felt the presence of a new element that blended us as we had never been blent before. My father had been one of the most successful men in the money-getting world: he had had no sentimental sufferings, no illness. The heaviest trouble that had befallen him was the death of his first wife. But he married my mother soon after; and I remember he seemed exactly the same, to my keen childish observation, the week after her death as before. But now, at last, a sorrow had come – the sorrow of old age, which suffers the more from the crushing of its pride and its hopes, in proportion as the pride and hope are narrow and prosaic. His son was to have been married soon – would probably have stood for the borough at the next election. That son's existence was the best motive that could be alleged for making new purchases of land every year to round off the estate. It is a dreary thing to live on doing the same things year after year, without knowing why we do them. Perhaps the tragedy of disappointed youth and passion is less piteous than the tragedy of disappointed age and worldliness.

As I saw into the desolation of my father's heart, I felt a movement of deep pity towards him, which was the beginning of a new affection – an affection that grew and strengthened in spite of the strange bitterness with which he regarded me in the first month or two after my brother's death. If it had not been for the softening influence of my compassion for him – the first deep compassion I had ever felt – I should have been stung by the perception that my father transferred the inheritance of an eldest son to me with a mortified sense that fate had compelled him to the unwelcome course of caring for me as an important being. It was only in spite of himself that he began to think of me with anxious regard. There is hardly any neglected child for whom death has made vacant a more favoured place, who will not understand what I mean.

Gradually, however, my new deference to his wishes, the effect of that patience which was born of my pity for him, won upon his affection, and he began to please himself with the endeavour to make me fill my brother's place as fully as my feebler personality would admit. I saw that the prospect which by-and-by presented itself of my becoming Bertha's husband was welcome to him, and he even contemplated in my case what he had not intended in my brother's – that his son and daughter-in-law should make one household with him. My softened feeling towards my father made this the happiest time I had known since childhood; – these last months in which I retained the delicious illusion of loving Bertha, of longing and doubting and hoping that she might love me. She behaved with a certain new consciousness and distance towards me after my brother's death; and I too was under a double constraint – that of delicacy towards my brother's memory, and of anxiety as to the impression my abrupt words had left on her mind. But the additional screen this mutual reserve erected between us only brought me more completely under her power: no matter how empty the adytum, so that the veil be thick enough. So absolute is our soul's need of something hidden and uncertain for the maintenance of that doubt and hope and effort which are the breath of its life, that if the whole future were laid bare to us beyond to-day, the interest of all mankind would be bent on the hours that lie between; we should pant after the uncertainties of our one morning and our one afternoon; we should rush fiercely to the Exchange for our last possibility of speculation, of success, of disappointment; we should have a glut of political prophets foretelling a crisis or a no-crisis within the only twenty-four hours left open to prophecy. Conceive the condition of the human mind if all propositions whatsoever were self-evident except one, which was to become self-evident at the close of a summer's day, but in the meantime might be the subject of question, of hypothesis,

47

of debate. Art and philosophy, literature and science, would fasten like bees on that one proposition which had the honey of probability in it, and be the more eager because their enjoyment would end with sunset. Our impulses, our spiritual activities, no more adjust themselves to the idea of their future nullity, than the beating of our heart, or the irritability of our muscles.

Bertha, the slim, fair-haired girl, whose present thoughts and emotions were an enigma to me amidst the fatiguing obviousness of the other minds around me, was as absorbing to me as a single unknown to-day – as a single hypothetic proposition to remain problematic till sunset; and all the cramped, hemmed-in belief and disbelief, trust and distrust, of my nature, welled out in this one narrow channel.

And she made me believe that she loved me. Without ever quitting her tone of *badinage* and playful superiority, she intoxicated me with the sense that I was necessary to her, that she was never at ease unless I was near her, submitting to her playful tyranny. It costs a woman so little effort to besot us in this way! A half-repressed word, a moment's unexpected silence, even an easy fit of petulance on our account, will serve us as *hashish* for a long while. Out of the subtlest web of scarcely perceptible signs, she set me weaving the fancy that she had always unconsciously loved me better than Alfred, but that, with the ignorant fluttered sensibility of a young girl, she had been imposed on by the charm that lay for her in the distinction of being admired and chosen by a man who made so brilliant a figure in the world as my brother. She satirised herself in a very graceful way for her vanity and ambition. What was it to me that I had the light of my wretched prevision on the fact that now it was I who possessed at least all but the personal part of my brother's advantages? Our sweet illusions are half of them conscious illusions, like effects of colour that we know to be made up of tinsel, broken glass, and rags.

We were married eighteen months after Alfred's death, one cold, clear morning in April, when there came hail and sunshine both together; and Bertha, in her white silk and pale-green leaves, and the pale hues of her hair and face, looked like the spirit of the morning. My father was happier than he had thought of being again: my marriage, he felt sure, would complete the desirable modification of my character, and make me practical and worldly enough to take my place in society among sane men. For he delighted in Bertha's tact and acuteness, and felt sure she would be mistress of me, and make me what she chose: I was only twenty-one, and madly in love with her. Poor father! He kept that hope a little while after our first year of marriage, and it was not quite extinct when paralysis came and saved him from utter disappointment.

I shall hurry through the rest of my story, not dwelling so much as I have hitherto done on my inward experience. When people are well known to each other, they talk rather of what befalls them externally, leaving their feelings and sentiments to be inferred.

We lived in a round of visits for some time after our return home, giving splendid dinner-parties, and making a sensation in our neighbourhood by the new lustre of our equipage, for my father had reserved this display of his increased wealth for the period of his son's marriage; and we gave our acquaintances liberal opportunity for remarking that it was a pity I made so poor a figure as an heir and a bridegroom. The nervous fatigue of this existence, the insincerities and platitudes which I had to live through twice over – through my inner and outward sense – would have been maddening to me, if I had not had that sort of intoxicated callousness which came from the delights of a first passion. A bride and bridegroom, surrounded by all the appliances of wealth, hurried through the day by the whirl of society, filling their solitary moments with hastily-snatched caresses, are prepared for their future life together as the novice is prepared for the cloister – by experiencing its utmost contrast.

Through all these crowded excited months, Bertha's inward self remained shrouded from me, and I still read her thoughts only through the language of her lips and demeanour: I had still the human interest of wondering whether what I did and said pleased her, of longing to hear a word of affection, of giving a delicious exaggeration of meaning to her smile. But I was conscious of a growing difference in her manner towards me; sometimes strong enough to be called haughty coldness, cutting and chilling me as the hail had done that came across the sunshine on our marriage morning; sometimes only perceptible in the dexterous avoidance of a *tête-à-tête* walk or dinner to which I had been looking forward. I had been deeply pained by this – had even felt a sort of crushing of the heart, from the sense that my brief day of happiness was near its setting; but still I remained dependent on Bertha, eager for the last rays of a bliss that would soon be gone for ever, hoping and watching for some after-glow more beautiful from the impending night.

I remember – how should I not remember? – the time when that dependence and hope utterly left me, when the sadness I had felt in Bertha's growing estrangement became a joy that I looked back upon with longing, as a man might look back on the last pains in a paralysed limb. It was just after the close of my father's last illness, which had necessarily withdrawn us from society and thrown us more upon each other. It was the evening of my father's death. On that evening the veil which had shrouded Bertha's soul from me – had made me find in her alone among my fellow-beings the blessed possibility of mystery, and doubt, and expectation – was first withdrawn. Perhaps it was the first day since the beginning of my passion for her, in which that passion was completely neutralised by the presence of an absorbing feeling of another kind. I had been watching by my father's deathbed: I had been witnessing the last fitful yearning glance his soul had cast back on the spent inheritance of life – the last faint consciousness of love he had gathered from the pressure of my hand. What are all our personal loves when we have been sharing in that supreme agony? In the first moments when we come away from the presence of death, every other relation to the living is merged, to our feeling, in the great relation of a common nature and a common destiny.

In that state of mind I joined Bertha in her private sitting-room. She was seated in a leaning posture on a settee, with her back towards the door; the great rich coils of her pale blond hair surmounting her small neck, visible above the back of the settee. I remember, as I closed the door behind me, a cold tremulousness seizing me, and a vague sense of being hated and lonely – vague and strong, like a presentiment. I know how I looked at that moment, for I saw myself in Bertha's thought as she lifted her cutting grey eyes, and looked at me: a miserable ghost-seer, surrounded by phantoms in the noonday, trembling under a breeze when the leaves were still, without appetite for the common objects of human desire, but pining after the moonbeams. We were front to front with each other, and judged each other. The terrible moment of complete illumination had come to me, and I saw that the darkness had hidden no landscape from me, but only a blank prosaic wall: from that evening forth, through the sickening years which followed, I saw all round the narrow room of this woman's soul – saw petty artifice and mere negation where I had delighted to believe in coy sensibilities and in wit at war with latent feeling – saw the light floating vanities of the girl defining themselves into the systematic coquetry, the scheming selfishness, of the woman – saw repulsion and antipathy harden into cruel hatred, giving pain only for the sake of wreaking itself.

For Bertha too, after her kind, felt the bitterness of disillusion. She had believed that my wild poet's passion for her would make me her slave; and that, being her slave, I should execute her will in all things. With the essential shallowness of a negative, unimaginative nature, she was unable to conceive the fact that sensibilities were anything else than weaknesses. She had thought my weaknesses would put me in her power, and she found them unmanageable forces. Our positions were reversed. Before marriage she had completely mastered my imagination, for she was a secret to me; and I created the unknown thought before which I trembled as if it were hers. But now that her soul was laid open to me, now that I was compelled to share the privacy of her motives, to follow all the petty devices that preceded her words and acts, she found herself powerless with me, except to produce in me the chill shudder of repulsion – powerless, because I could be acted on by no lever within her reach. I was dead to worldly ambitions, to social vanities, to all the incentives within the compass of her narrow imagination, and I lived under influences utterly invisible to her.

She was really pitiable to have such a husband, and so

all the world thought. A graceful, brilliant woman, like Bertha, who smiled on morning callers, made a figure in ball-rooms, and was capable of that light repartee which, from such a woman, is accepted as wit, was secure of carrying off all sympathy from a husband who was sickly, abstracted, and, as some suspected, crack-brained. Even the servants in our house gave her the balance of their regard and pity. For there were no audible quarrels between us; our alienation, our repulsion from each other, lay within the silence of our own hearts; and if the mistress went out a great deal, and seemed to dislike the master's society, was it not natural, poor thing? The master was odd. I was kind and just to my dependants, but I excited in them a shrinking, half-contemptuous pity; for this class of men and women are but slightly determined in their estimate of others by general considerations, or even experience, of character. They judge of persons as they judge of coins, and value those who pass current at a high rate.

After a time I interfered so little with Bertha's habits, that it might seem wonderful how her hatred towards me could grow so intense and active as it did. But she had begun to suspect, by some involuntary betrayals of mine, that there was an abnormal power of penetration in me – that fitfully, at least, I was strangely cognisant of her thoughts and intentions, and she began to be haunted by a terror of me, which alternated every now and then with defiance. She meditated continually how the incubus could be shaken off her life – how she could be freed from this hateful bond to a being whom she at once despised as an imbecile, and dreaded as an inquisitor. For a long while she lived in the hope that my evident wretchedness would drive me to the commission of suicide; but suicide was not in my nature. I was too completely swayed by the sense that I was in the grasp of unknown forces, to believe in my power of self-release. Towards my own destiny I had become entirely passive; for my one ardent desire had spent itself, and impulse no longer predominated over knowledge. For this reason I never thought of taking any steps towards a complete separation, which would have made our alienation evident to the world. Why should I rush for help to a new course, when I was only suffering from the consequences of a deed which had been the act of my intensest will? That would have been the logic of one who had desires to gratify, and I had no desires. But Bertha and I lived more and more aloof from each other. The rich find it easy to live married and apart.

That course of our life which I have indicated in a few sentences filled the space of years. So much misery – so slow and hideous a growth of hatred and sin, may be compressed into a sentence! And men judge of each other's lives through this summary medium. They epitomise the experience of their fellow-mortal, and pronounce judgment on him in neat syntax, and feel themselves wise and virtuous – conquerors over the temptations they define in well-selected predicates. Seven years of wretchedness glide glibly over the lips of the man who has never counted them out in moments of chill disappointment, of head and heart throbbings, of dread and vain wrestling, of remorse and despair. We learn *words* by rote, but not their meaning; *that* must be paid for with our life-blood, and printed in the subtle fibres of our nerves.

But I will hasten to finish my story. Brevity is justified at once to those who readily understand, and to those who will never understand.

Some years after my father's death, I was sitting by the dim firelight in my library one January evening – sitting in the leather chair that used to be my father's – when Bertha appeared at the door, with a candle in her hand, and advanced towards me. I knew the ball-dress she had on – the white ball-dress, with the green jewels, shone upon by the light of the wax candle which lit up the medallion of the dying Cleopatra on the mantelpiece. Why did she come to me before going out? I had not seen her in the library, which was my habitual place, for months. Why did she stand before me with the candle in her hand, with her cruel contemptuous eyes fixed on me, and the glittering serpent, like a familiar demon, on her breast? For a moment I thought this fulfilment of my vision at Vienna marked some dreadful crisis in my fate, but I saw nothing in Bertha's mind, as she stood before me, except scorn for the look of overwhelming misery with which I sat before her . . . 'Fool, idiot, why don't you kill yourself, then?' – that was her thought. But at length her thoughts reverted to her errand, and she spoke aloud. The apparently indifferent nature of the errand seemed to make a ridiculous anticlimax to my prevision and my agitation.

'I have had to hire a new maid. Fletcher is going to be married, and she wants me to ask you to let her husband have the public-house and farm at Molton. I wish him to have it. You must give the promise now, because Fletcher is going to-morrow morning – and quickly, because I'm in a hurry.'

'Very well; you may promise her,' I said, indifferently, and Bertha swept out of the library again.

I always shrank from the sight of a new person, and all the more when it was a person whose mental life was likely to weary my reluctant insight with worldly ignorant trivialities. But I shrank especially from the sight of this new maid, because her advent had been announced to me at a moment to which I could not cease to attach some fatality: I had a vague dread that I should find her mixed up with the dreary drama of my life – that some new sickening vision would reveal her to me as an evil genius. When at last I did unavoidably meet her, the vague dread was changed into definite disgust. She was a tall, wiry, dark-eyed woman, this Mrs Archer, with a face handsome enough to give her coarse hard nature the odious finish of bold, self-confident coquetry. That was enough to make me avoid her, quite apart from the contemptuous feeling

with which she contemplated me. I seldom saw her; but
I perceived that she rapidly became a favourite with her
mistress, and, after the lapse of eight or nine months, I
began to be aware that there had arisen in Bertha's mind
towards this woman a mingled feeling of fear and dependence, and that this feeling was associated with ill-defined
images of candle-light scenes in her dressing-room, and
the looking-up of something in Bertha's cabinet. My
interviews with my wife had become so brief and so rarely
solitary, that I had no opportunity of perceiving these
images in her mind with more definiteness. The recollec-
tions of the past become contracted in the rapidity of
thought till they sometimes bear hardly a more distinct resemblance to the external reality than the forms
of an oriental alphabet to the objects that suggested
them.

Besides, for the last year or more a modification had been
going forward in my mental condition, and was growing
more and more marked. My insight into the minds of
those around me was becoming dimmer and more fitful,
and the ideas that crowded my double consciousness became less and less dependent on any personal contact.
All that was personal in me seemed to be suffering a
gradual death, so that I was losing the organ through
which the personal agitations and projects of others could
affect me. But along with this relief from wearisome insight,
there was a new development of what I concluded – as I
have since found rightly – to be a prevision of external

scenes. It was as if the relation between me and my fellow-men was more and more deadened, and my relation to what we call the inanimate was quickened into new life. The more I lived apart from society, and in proportion as my wretchedness subsided from the violent throb of agonised passion into the dulness of habitual pain, the more frequent and vivid became such visions as that I had had of Prague – of strange cities, of sandy plains, of gigantic ruins, of midnight skies with strange bright constellations, of mountain-passes, of grassy nooks flecked with the afternoon sunshine through the boughs: I was in the midst of such scenes, and in all of them one presence seemed to weigh on me in all these mighty shapes – the presence of something unknown and pitiless. For continual suffering had annihilated religious faith within me: to the utterly miserable – the unloving and the unloved – there is no religion possible, no worship but a worship of devils. And beyond all these, and continually recurring, was the vision of my death – the pangs, the suffocation, the last struggle, when life would be grasped at in vain.

Things were in this state near the end of the seventh year. I had become entirely free from insight, from my abnormal cognisance of any other consciousness than my own, and instead of intruding involuntarily into the world of other minds, was living continually in my own solitary future. Bertha was aware that I was greatly changed. To my surprise she had of late seemed to seek

opportunities of remaining in my society, and had culti-
vated that kind of distant yet familiar talk which is
customary between a husband and wife who live in polite
and irrevocable alienation. I bore this with languid sub-
mission, and without feeling enough interest in her
motives to be roused into keen observation; yet I could
not help perceiving something triumphant and excited
in her carriage and the expression of her face – something
too subtle to express itself in words or tones, but giving
one the idea that she lived in a state of expectation or
hopeful suspense. My chief feeling was satisfaction that
her inner self was once more shut out from me; and I
almost revelled for the moment in the absent melancholy
that made me answer her at cross purposes, and betray
utter ignorance of what she had been saying. I remember
well the look and the smile with which she one day said,
after a mistake of this kind on my part: 'I used to think
you were a clairvoyant and that was the reason why you
were so bitter against other clairvoyants, wanting to keep
your monopoly; but I see now you have become rather
duller than the rest of the world.'

I said nothing in reply. It occurred to me that her
recent obtrusion of herself upon me might have been
prompted by the wish to test my power of detecting some
of her secrets; but I let the thought drop again at once:
her motives and her deeds had no interest for me, and
whatever pleasures she might be seeking, I had no wish
to balk her. There was still pity in my soul for every living

thing, and Bertha was living – was surrounded with possibilities of misery.

Just at this time there occurred an event which roused me somewhat from my inertia, and gave me an interest in the passing moment that I had thought impossible for me. It was a visit from Charles Meunier, who had written me word that he was coming to England for relaxation from too strenuous labour, and would like to see me. Meunier had now a European reputation; but his letter to me expressed that keen remembrance of an early regard, an early debt of sympathy, which is inseparable from nobility of character: and I too felt as if his presence would be to me like a transient resurrection into a happier pre-existence.

He came, and as far as possible, I renewed our old pleasure of making *tête-à-tête* excursions, though, instead of mountains and glaciers and the wide blue lake, we had to content ourselves with mere slopes and ponds and artificial plantations. The years had changed us both, but with what different result! Meunier was now a brilliant figure in society, to whom elegant women pretended to listen, and whose acquaintance was boasted of by noblemen ambitious of brains. He repressed with the utmost delicacy all betrayal of the shock which I am sure he must have received from our meeting, or of a desire to penetrate into my condition and circumstances, and sought by the utmost exertion of his charming social powers to make our reunion agreeable. Bertha was much struck by the unexpected fascinations of a visitor whom she had expected to find presentable only on the score of his celebrity, and put forth all her coquetries and accomplishments. Apparently she succeeded in attracting his admiration, for his manner towards her was attentive and flattering. The effect of his presence on me was so benignant, especially in those renewals of our old *tête-à-tête* wanderings, when he poured forth to me wonderful narratives of his professional experience, that more than once, when his talk turned on the psychological relations of disease, the thought crossed my mind that, if his stay with me were long enough, I might possibly bring myself to tell this man the secrets of my lot. Might there not lie some remedy for *me*, too, in his science? Might there not at least lie some comprehension and sympathy ready for me in his large and susceptible mind? But the thought only flickered feebly now and then, and died out before it could become a wish. The horror I had of again breaking in on the privacy of another soul, made me, by an irrational instinct, draw the shroud of concealment more closely around my own, as we automatically perform the gesture we feel to be wanting in another.

When Meunier's visit was approaching its conclusion, there happened an event which caused some excitement in our household, owing to the surprisingly strong effect it appeared to produce on Bertha – on Bertha, the self-possessed, who usually seemed inaccessible to feminine agitations, and did even her hate in a self-restrained hygienic manner. This event was the sudden severe illness of her maid, Mrs Archer. I have reserved to this moment the mention of a circumstance which had forced itself on my notice shortly before Meunier's arrival, namely, that there had been some quarrel between Bertha and this maid, apparently during a visit to a distant family, in which she had accompanied her mistress. I had overheard Archer speaking in a tone of bitter insolence, which I should have thought an adequate reason for immediate dismissal. No dismissal followed; on the contrary, Bertha seemed to be silently putting up with personal inconveniences from the exhibitions of this woman's temper. I was the more astonished to observe that her illness seemed a cause of strong solicitude to Bertha; that she was at the bedside night and day, and would allow no one else to officiate as head-nurse. It happened that our family doctor was out on a holiday, an accident which made Meunier's presence in the house doubly welcome, and he apparently entered into the case with an interest which seemed so much stronger than the ordinary professional feeling, that one day when he had fallen into a long fit of silence after visiting her, I said to him –

'Is this a very peculiar case of disease, Meunier?'

'No,' he answered, 'it is an attack of peritonitis, which will be fatal, but which does not differ physically from many other cases that have come under my observation. But I'll tell you what I have on my mind. I want to make

63

an experiment on this woman, if you will give me permission. It can do her no harm – will give her no pain – for I shall not make it until life is extinct to all purposes of sensation. I want to try the effect of transfusing blood into her arteries after the heart has ceased to beat for some minutes. I have tried the experiment again and again with animals that have died of this disease, with astounding results, and I want to try it on a human subject. I have the small tubes necessary, in a case I have with me, and the rest of the apparatus could be prepared readily. I should use my own blood – take it from my own arm. This woman won't live through the night, I'm convinced, and I want you to promise me your assistance in making the experiment. I can't do without another hand, but it would perhaps not be well to call in a medical assistant from among your provincial doctors. A disagreeable foolish version of the thing might get abroad.'

'Have you spoken to my wife on the subject?' I said, 'because she appears to be peculiarly sensitive about this woman: she has been a favourite maid.'

'To tell you the truth,' said Meunier, 'I don't want her to know about it. There are always insuperable difficulties with women in these matters, and the effect on the supposed dead body may be startling. You and I will sit up together, and be in readiness. When certain symptoms appear I shall take you in, and at the right moment we must manage to get every one else out of the room.'

64

I need not give our farther conversation on the subject. He entered very fully into the details, and overcame my repulsion from them, by exciting in me a mingled awe and curiosity concerning the possible results of his experiment.

We prepared everything, and he instructed me in my part as assistant. He had not told Bertha of his absolute conviction that Archer would not survive through the night, and endeavoured to persuade her to leave the patient and take a night's rest. But she was obstinate, suspecting the fact that death was at hand, and supposing that he wished merely to save her nerves. She refused to leave the sick-room. Meunier and I sat up together in the library, he making frequent visits to the sick-room, and returning with the information that the case was taking precisely the course he expected. Once he said to me, 'Can you imagine any cause of ill feeling this woman has against her mistress, who is so devoted to her?'

'I think there was some misunderstanding between them before her illness. Why do you ask?'

'Because I have observed for the last five or six hours – since, I fancy, she has lost all hope of recovery – there seems a strange prompting in her to say something which pain and failing strength forbid her to utter; and there is a look of hideous meaning in her eyes, which she turns continually towards her mistress. In this disease the mind often remains singularly clear to the last.'

'I am not surprised at an indication of malevolent

feeling in her,' I said. 'She is a woman who has always inspired me with distrust and dislike, but she managed to insinuate herself into her mistress's favour.' He was silent after this, looking at the fire with an air of absorption, till he went up-stairs again. He stayed away longer than usual, and on returning, said to me quietly, 'Come now.'

I followed him to the chamber where death was hovering. The dark hangings of the large bed made a background that gave a strong relief to Bertha's pale face as I entered. She started forward as she saw me enter, and then looked at Meunier with an expression of angry inquiry; but he lifted up his hand as if to impose silence, while he fixed his glance on the dying woman and felt her pulse. The face was pinched and ghastly, a cold perspiration was on the forehead, and the eyelids were lowered so as almost to conceal the large dark eyes. After a minute or two, Meunier walked round to the other side of the bed where Bertha stood, and with his usual air of gentle politeness towards her begged her to leave the patient under our care – everything should be done for her – she was no longer in a state to be conscious of an affectionate presence. Bertha was hesitating, apparently almost willing to believe his assurance and to comply. She looked round at the ghastly dying face, as if to read the confirmation of that assurance, when for a moment the lowered eyelids were raised again, and it seemed as if the eyes were looking towards Bertha, but blankly. A shudder passed through

Bertha's frame, and she returned to her station near the pillow, tacitly implying that she would not leave the room.

The eyelids were lifted no more. Once I looked at Bertha as she watched the face of the dying one. She wore a rich *peignoir*, and her blond hair was half covered by a lace cap: in her attire she was, as always, an elegant woman, fit to figure in a picture of modern aristocratic life: but I asked myself how that face of hers could ever have seemed to me the face of a woman born of woman, with memories of childhood, capable of pain, needing to be fondled? The features at that moment seemed so pre-ternaturally sharp, the eyes were so hard and eager – she looked like a cruel immortal, finding her spiritual feast in the agonies of a dying race. For across those hard features there came something like a flash when the last hour had been breathed out, and we all felt that the dark veil had completely fallen. What secret was there between Bertha and this woman? I turned my eyes from her with a horrible dread lest my insight should return, and I should be obliged to see what had been breeding about two unloving women's hearts. I felt that Bertha had been watching for the moment of death as the sealing of her secret: I thanked Heaven it could remain sealed for me.

Meunier said quietly, 'She is gone.' He then gave his arm to Bertha, and she submitted to be led out of the room.

I suppose it was at her order that two female attendants came into the room, and dismissed the younger one who had been present before. When they entered, Meunier had already opened the artery in the long thin neck that lay rigid on the pillow, and I dismissed them, ordering them to remain at a distance till we rang: the doctor, I said, had an operation to perform – he was not sure about the death. For the next twenty minutes I forgot everything but Meunier and the experiment in which he was so absorbed, that I think his senses would have been closed against all sounds or sights which had no relation to it. It was my task at first to keep up the artificial respiration in the body after the transfusion had been effected, but presently Meunier relieved me, and I could see the wondrous slow return of life; the breast began to heave, the inspirations became stronger, the eyelids quivered, and the soul seemed to have returned beneath them. The artificial respiration was withdrawn: still the breathing continued, and there was a movement of the lips.

Just then I heard the handle of the door moving: I suppose Bertha had heard from the women that they had been dismissed: probably a vague fear had arisen in her mind, for she entered with a look of alarm. She came to the foot of the bed and gave a stifled cry.

The dead woman's eyes were·wide open, and met hers in full recognition – the recognition of hate. With a sudden strong effort, the hand that Bertha had thought for ever still was pointed towards her, and the haggard face moved. The gasping eager voice said –

'You mean to poison your husband . . . the poison is

in the black cabinet . . . I got it for you . . . you laughed at me, and told lies about me behind my back, to make me disgusting . . . because you were jealous . . . are you sorry . . . now?'

The lips continued to murmur, but the sounds were no longer distinct. Soon there was no sound – only a slight movement: the flame had leaped out, and was being extinguished the faster. The wretched woman's heart-strings had been set to hatred and vengeance; the spirit of life had swept the chords for an instant, and was gone again for ever. Great God! Is this what it is to live again . . . to wake up with our unstilled thirst upon us, with our unuttered curses rising to our lips, with our muscles ready to act out their half-committed sins?

Bertha stood pale at the foot of the bed, quivering and helpless, despairing of devices, like a cunning animal whose hiding-places are surrounded by swift-advancing flame. Even Meunier looked paralysed; life for that moment ceased to be a scientific problem to him. As for me, this scene seemed of one texture with the rest of my existence: horror was my familiar, and this new revelation was only like an old pain recurring with new circumstances.

Since then Bertha and I have lived apart – she in her own neighbourhood, the mistress of half our wealth, I as a wanderer in foreign countries, until I came to this Devonshire nest to die. Bertha lives pitied and admired; for what had I against that charming woman, whom every one but myself could have been happy with? There had been no witness of the scene in the dying room except Meunier, and while Meunier lived his lips were sealed by a promise to me.

Once or twice, weary of wandering, I rested in a favourite spot, and my heart went out towards the men and women and children whose faces were becoming familiar to me: but I was driven away again in terror at the approach of my old insight – driven away to live continually with the one Unknown Presence revealed and yet hidden by the moving curtain of the earth and sky. Till at last disease took hold of me and forced me to rest here – forced me to live in dependence on my servants. And then the curse of insight – of my double consciousness, came again, and has never left me. I know all their narrow thoughts, their feeble regard, their half-wearied pity.

It is the 20th of September 1850. I know these figures I have just written, as if they were a long familiar inscription. I have seen them on this page in my desk unnumbered times, when the scene of my dying struggle has opened upon me . . .

(1859.)

SILLY NOVELS BY
LADY NOVELISTS

Silly novels by Lady Novelists are a genus with many species, determined by the particular quality of silliness that predominates in them – the frothy, the prosy, the pious, or the pedantic. But it is a mixture of all these – a composite order of feminine fatuity, that produces the largest class of such novels, which we shall distinguish as the *mind-and-millinery* species. The heroine is usually an heiress, probably a peeress in her own right, with perhaps a vicious baronet, an amiable duke, and an irresistible younger son of a marquis as lovers in the foreground, a clergyman and a poet sighing for her in the middle distance, and a crowd of undefined adorers dimly indicated beyond. Her eyes and her wit are both dazzling; her nose and her morals are alike free from any tendency to irregularity; she has a superb *contralto* and a superb intellect; she is perfectly well-dressed and perfectly religious; she dances like a sylph, and reads the Bible in the original tongues. Or it may be that the heroine is not an heiress – that rank and wealth are the only things in which she is deficient; but she infallibly gets into high society, she has the triumph of refusing many matches and securing the best, and she wears some family jewels or other as a sort of crown of righteousness at the end. Rakish men either bite their lips in impotent confusion at her repartees, or are touched to penitence by her reproofs, which, on appropriate occasions, rise to a lofty strain of rhetoric; indeed, there is a general propensity in her to make speeches, and to rhapsodize at some length when she retires to her bedroom. In her recorded conversations she is amazingly eloquent, and in her unrecorded conversations, amazingly witty. She is understood to have a depth of insight that looks through and through the shallow theories of philosophers, and her superior instincts are a sort of dial by which men have only to set their clocks and watches, and all will go well. The men play a very subordinate part by her side. You are consoled now and then by a hint that they have affairs, which keeps you in mind that the working-day business of the world is somehow being carried on, but ostensibly the final cause of their existence is that they may accompany the heroine on her 'starring' expedition through life. They see her at a ball, and are dazzled; at a flower-show, and they are fascinated; on a riding excursion, and they are witched by her noble horsemanship; at church, and they are awed by the sweet solemnity of her demeanour. She is the ideal woman in feelings, faculties, and flounces. For all this, she as often as not marries the wrong person to begin with, and she suffers terribly from the plots and intrigues of the vicious baronet; but even death has a soft place in his heart for such a paragon, and remedies all mistakes for her just at the right moment. The vicious baronet is sure to be killed in a duel, and the tedious husband dies in his bed, requesting his wife, as a particular favour to him, to marry the man she loves best, and having already dispatched a note to the lover informing him of the comfortable arrangement. Before matters arrive at this desirable issue our feelings are tried by seeing the noble, lovely, and gifted heroine pass through many *mauvais moments*, but we have the satisfaction of knowing that her sorrows are wept into embroidered pocket-handkerchiefs, that her fainting form reclines on the very best upholstery, and that whatever vicissitudes she may undergo, from being dashed out of her carriage to having her head shaved in a fever, she comes out of them all with a complexion more blooming and locks more redundant than ever.

We may remark, by the way, that we have been relieved from a serious scruple by discovering that silly novels by lady novelists rarely introduce us into any other than very lofty and fashionable society. We had imagined that destitute women turned novelists, as they turned governesses, because they had no other 'lady-like' means of getting their bread. On this supposition, vacillating syntax and improbable incident had a certain pathos for us, like the extremely supererogatory pincushions and ill-devised nightcaps that are offered for sale by a blind man. We felt the commodity to be a nuisance, but we were glad to think that the money went to relieve the necessitous, and we pictured to ourselves lonely women struggling for a maintenance, or wives and daughters devoting themselves to the production of 'copy' out of pure heroism, – perhaps to pay their husband's debts, or to purchase luxuries for a sick father. Under these impressions we shrank from criticizing a lady's novel: her English might be faulty, but, we said to ourselves, her motives are irreproachable; her imagination may be uninventive, but her patience is untiring. Empty writing was excused by an empty stomach, and twaddle was consecrated by tears. But no! This theory of ours, like many other pretty theories, has had to give way before observation. Women's silly novels, we are now convinced, are written under totally different circumstances. The fair writers have evidently never talked to a tradesman except from a carriage window; they have no notion of the working classes except as 'dependants'; they think £500 a year a miserable pittance; Belgravia and 'baronial halls' are their primary truths; and they have no idea of feeling interest in any man who is not at least a great landed proprietor, if not a prime minister. It is clear that they write in elegant boudoirs, with violet-coloured ink and a ruby pen; that they must be entirely indifferent to publishers' accounts, and inexperienced in every form of poverty except poverty of brains. It is true that we are constantly struck with the want of verisimilitude in their representations of the high society in which they seem to live; but then they betray no closer acquaintance with any other form of life. If their peers and peeresses are improbable, their literary men, tradespeople, and cottagers are impossible; and their intellect seems to have the peculiar impartiality of reproducing both what they *have* seen and heard, and what they have *not* seen and heard, with equal unfaithfulness.

There are few women, we suppose, who have not seen something of children under five years of age, yet in *Compensation*, a recent novel of the mind-and-millinery species, which calls itself a 'story of real life', we have a child of four and a half years old talking in this Ossianic fashion: –

'Oh, I am so happy, dear gran'mamma; – I have seen, – I have seen such a delightful person: he is like everything beautiful, – like the smell of sweet flowers, and the view from Ben Lomond; – or no, *better than that* – he is like what I think of and see when I am very, very happy; and he is really like mamma, too, when she sings; and his forehead is like *that distant sea*,' she continued, pointing to the blue Mediterranean; 'there seems no end – no end; or like the clusters of stars I like best to look at on a warm fine night . . . Don't look so . . . your forehead is like Loch Lomond, when the wind is blowing and the sun is gone in; I like the sunshine best when the lake is smooth . . . So now – I like it better than ever . . . it is more beautiful still from the dark cloud that has gone over it, *when the sun*

suddenly lights up all the colours of the forests and shining purple
rocks, and it is all reflected in the waters below.'

We are not surprised to learn that the mother of this
infant phenomenon, who exhibits symptoms so alarm-
ingly like those of adolescence repressed by gin, is herself
a phœnix. We are assured, again and again, that she had
a remarkably original mind, that she was a genius, and
'conscious of her originality', and she was fortunate
enough to have a lover who was also a genius, and a man
of 'most original mind'.

This lover, we read, though 'wonderfully similar' to her
'in powers and capacity', was 'infinitely superior to her
in faith and development', and she saw in him the
'"Agape" – so rare to find – of which she had read and
admired the meaning in her Greek Testament; having,
from her great facility in learning languages, read the Scrip-
tures in their original *tongues*.' Of course! Greek and
Hebrew are mere play to a heroine; Sanscrit is no more
than *a b c* to her; and she can talk with perfect correctness
in any language except English. She is a polking poly-
glot, a Creuzer in crinoline. Poor men! There are so few
of you who know even Hebrew; you think it something
to boast of if, like Bolingbroke, you only 'understand that
sort of learning, and what is writ about it'; and you are
perhaps adoring women who can think slightingly of you
in all the Semitic languages successively. But, then, as
we are almost invariably told, that a heroine has a

'beautifully small head', and as her intellect has probably been early invigorated by an attention to costume and deportment, we may conclude that she can pick up the Oriental tongues, to say nothing of their dialects, with the same aërial facility that the butterfly sips nectar. Besides, there can be no difficulty in conceiving the depth of the heroine's erudition, when that of the authoress is so evident.

In *Laura Gay*, another novel of the same school, the heroine seems less at home in Greek and Hebrew, but she makes up for the deficiency by a quite playful familiarity with the Latin classics – with the 'dear old Virgil', 'the graceful Horace, the humane Cicero, and the pleasant Livy'; indeed, it is such a matter of course with her to quote Latin, that she does it at a picnic in a very mixed company of ladies and gentlemen, having, we are told, 'no conception that the nobler sex were capable of jealousy on this subject. And if, indeed,' continues the biographer of Laura Gay, 'the wisest and noblest portion of that sex were in the majority, no such sentiment would exist; but while Miss Wyndhams and Mr Redfords abound, great sacrifices must be made to their existence.' Such sacrifices, we presume, as abstaining from Latin quotations, of extremely moderate interest and applicability, which the wise and noble minority of the other sex would be quite as willing to dispense with as the foolish and ignoble majority. It is as little the custom of well-bred men as of well-bred women to quote Latin in mixed parties; they can contain their familiarity with 'the humane Cicero' without allowing it to boil over in ordinary conversation, and even references to 'the pleasant Livy' are not absolutely irrepressible. But Ciceronian Latin is the mildest form of Miss Gay's conversational power. Being on the Palatine with a party of sightseers, she falls into the following vein of well-rounded remark: –

> Truth can only be pure objectively, for even in the creeds where it predominates, being subjective, and parcelled out into portions, each of these necessarily receives a hue of idiosyncrasy, that is, a taint of superstition more or less strong; while in such creeds as the Roman Catholic, ignorance, interest, the bias of ancient idolatries, and the force of authority, have gradually accumulated on the pure truth, and transformed it, at last, into a mass of superstition for the majority of its votaries; and how few are there, alas! whose zeal, courage, and intellectual energy are equal to the analysis of this accumulation, and to the discovery of the pearl of great price which lies hidden beneath this heap of rubbish.

We have often met with women much more novel and profound in their observations than Laura Gay, but rarely with any so inopportunely long-winded. A clerical lord, who is half in love with her, is alarmed by the daring remarks just quoted, and begins to suspect that she is inclined to free-thinking. But he is mistaken; when in a moment of sorrow he delicately begs leave to 'recall to her

memory, a *dépôt* of strength and consolation under affliction, which, until we are hard pressed by the trials of life,
we are too apt to forget', we learn that she really has
'recurrence to that sacred *dépôt*', together with the teapot.
There is a certain flavour of orthodoxy mixed with the
parade of fortunes and fine carriages in *Laura Gay*, but it
is an orthodoxy mitigated by study of 'the humane Cicero', and by an 'intellectual disposition to analyse'.

Compensation is much more heavily dosed with doc-
trine, but then it has a treble amount of snobbish
worldliness and absurd incident to tickle the palate of
pious frivolity. Linda, the heroine, is still more speculative and spiritual than Laura Gay, but she has been
'presented', and has more, and far grander, lovers; very
wicked and fascinating women are introduced – even a
French *lionne*; and no expense is spared to get up as
exciting a story as you will find in the most immoral
novels. In fact, it is a wonderful *pot pourri* of Almack's,
Scotch second-sight, Mr Rogers's breakfasts, Italian brig-
ands, death-bed conversions, superior authoresses, Italian
mistresses, and attempts at poisoning old ladies, the
whole served up with a garnish of talk about 'faith and
development', and 'most original minds'. Even Miss
Susan Barton, the superior authoress, whose pen moves
in a 'quick decided manner when she is composing',
declines the finest opportunities of marriage; and though
old enough to be Linda's mother (since we are told that
she refused Linda's father), has her hand sought by a

young earl, the heroine's rejected lover. Of course, genius and morality must be backed by eligible offers, or they would seem rather a dull affair; and piety, like other things, in order to be *comme il faut*, must be in 'society', and have admittance to the best circles.

Rank and Beauty is a more frothy and less religious variety of the mind-and-millinery species. The heroine, we are told, 'if she inherited her father's pride of birth and her mother's beauty of person, had in herself a tone of enthusiastic feeling that perhaps belongs to her age even in the lowly born, but which is refined into the high spirit of wild romance only in the far descended, who feel that it is their best inheritance'. This enthusiastic young lady, by dint of reading the newspaper to her father, falls in love with the *prime minister*, who, through the medium of leading articles and 'the *résumé* of the debates', shines upon her imagination as a bright particular star, which has no parallax for her, living in the country as simple Miss Wyndham. But she forthwith becomes Baroness Umfraville in her own right, astonishes the world with her beauty and accomplishments when she bursts upon it from her mansion in Spring Gardens, and, as you foresee, will presently come into contact with the unseen *objet aimé*. Perhaps the words 'prime minister' suggest to you a wrinkled or obese sexagenarian; but pray dismiss the image. Lord Rupert Conway has been 'called while still almost a youth to the first situation which a subject can hold in the *universe*', and even leading articles and a *résumé* of the debates have not conjured up a dream that surpasses the fact.

> The door opened again, and Lord Rupert Conway entered. Evelyn gave one glance. It was enough; she was not disappointed. It seemed as if a picture on which she had long gazed was suddenly instinct with life, and had stepped from its frame before her. His tall figure, the distinguished simplicity of his air – it was a living Vandyke, a cavalier, one of his noble cavalier ancestors, or one to whom her fancy had always likened him, who long of yore had, with an Umfraville, fought the Paynim far beyond sea. Was this reality?

Very little like it, certainly.

By and by, it becomes evident that the ministerial heart is touched. Lady Umfraville is on a visit to the Queen at Windsor, and, –

> The last evening of her stay, when they returned from riding, Mr Wyndham took her and a large party to the top of the Keep, to see the view. She was leaning on the battlements, gazing from that 'stately height' at the prospect beneath her, when Lord Rupert was by her side. 'What an unrivalled view!' exclaimed she.
>
> 'Yes, it would have been wrong to go without having been up here. You are pleased with your visit?'
>
> 'Enchanted! "A Queen to live and die under", to live and die for!'

'Ha!' cried he, with sudden emotion, and with a *eureka*
expression of countenance, as if he had *indeed found a heart
in unison with his own.*

The '*eureka* expression of countenance', you see at once
to be prophetic of marriage at the end of the third volume; but before that desirable consummation, there are
very complicated misunderstandings, arising chiefly from
the vindictive plotting of Sir Luttrell Wycherley, who is
a genius, a poet, and in every way a most remarkable
character indeed. He is not only a romantic poet, but a
hardened rake and a cynical wit; yet his deep passion for
Lady Umfraville has so impoverished his epigrammatic
talent, that he cuts an extremely poor figure in conversation. When she rejects him, he rushes into the shrubbery,
and rolls himself in the dirt; and on recovering, devotes
himself to the most diabolical and laborious schemes of
vengeance, in the course of which he disguises himself
as a quack physician, and enters into general practice,
foreseeing that Evelyn will fall ill, and that he shall be
called in to attend her. At last, when all his schemes are
frustrated, he takes leave of her in a long letter, written,
as you will perceive from the following passage, entirely
in the style of an eminent literary man: –

Oh, lady, nursed in pomp and pleasure, will you ever cast
one thought upon the miserable being who addresses you?
Will you ever, as your gilded galley is floating down the
unruffled stream of prosperity, will you ever, while lulled

by the sweetest music – thine own praises, – hear the far-off sigh from that world to which I am going?

On the whole, however, frothy as it is, we rather prefer *Rank and Beauty* to the two other novels we have mentioned. The dialogue is more natural and spirited; there is some frank ignorance, and no pedantry; and you are allowed to take the heroine's astounding intellect upon trust, without being called on to read her conversational refutations of sceptics and philosophers, or her rhetorical solutions of the mysteries of the universe.

Writers of the mind-and-millinery school are remarkably unanimous in their choice of diction. In their novels, there is usually a lady or gentleman who is more or less of a upas tree: the lover has a manly breast; minds are redolent of various things; hearts are hollow; events are utilized; friends are consigned to the tomb; infancy is an engaging period; the sun is a luminary that goes to his western couch, or gathers the rain-drops into his refulgent bosom; life is a melancholy boon; Albion and Scotia are conversational epithets. There is a striking resemblance, too, in the character of their moral comments, such, for instance, as that 'It is a fact, no less true than melancholy, that all people, more or less, richer or poorer, are swayed by bad example'; that 'Books, however trivial, contain some subjects from which useful information may be drawn'; that 'Vice can too often borrow the language of virtue'; that 'Merit and nobility of nature must exist, to be accepted, for clamour and pretension cannot impose upon those too well read in human nature to be easily deceived'; and that, 'In order to forgive, we must have been injured'. There is, doubtless, a class of readers to whom these remarks appear peculiarly pointed and pungent; for we often find them doubly and trebly scored with the pencil, and delicate hands giving in their determined adhesion to these hardy novelties by a distinct *très vrai*, emphasized by many notes of exclamation. The colloquial style of these novels is often marked by much ingenious inversion, and a careful avoidance of such cheap phraseology as can be heard every day. Angry young gentlemen exclaim – ''Tis ever thus, methinks'; and in the half hour before dinner a young lady informs her next neighbour that the first day she read Shakspeare she 'stole away into the park, and beneath the shadow of the greenwood tree, devoured with rapture the inspired page of the great magician'. But the most remarkable efforts of the mind-and-millinery writers lie in their philosophic reflections. The authoress of *Laura Gay*, for example, having married her hero and heroine, improves the event by observing that 'if those sceptics, whose eyes have so long gazed on matter that they can no longer see aught else in man, could once enter with heart and soul into such bliss as this, they would come to say that the soul of man and the polypus are not of common origin, or of the same texture'. Lady novelists, it appears, can see something else besides matter; they are not limited to phenomena, but can relieve their eye-sight by occasional glimpses of the *noumenon*, and are, therefore, naturally better able than any one else to confound sceptics, even of that remarkable, but to us unknown school, which maintains that the soul of man is of the same texture as the polypus.

The most pitiable of all silly novels by lady novelists are what we may call the *oracular* species – novels intended to expound the writer's religious, philosophical, or moral theories. There seems to be a notion abroad among women, rather akin to the superstition that the speech and actions of idiots are inspired, and that the human being most entirely exhausted of common sense is the fittest vehicle of revelation. To judge from their writings, there are certain ladies who think that an amazing ignorance, both of science and of life, is the best possible qualification for forming an opinion on the knottiest moral and speculative questions. Apparently, their recipe for solving all such difficulties is something like this: – Take a woman's head, stuff it with a smattering of philosophy and literature chopped small, and with false notions of society baked hard, let it hang over a desk a few hours every day, and serve up hot in feeble English, when not required. You will rarely meet with a lady novelist of the oracular class who is diffident of her ability to decide on theological questions, – who has any suspicion that she is not capable of discriminating with the nicest accuracy between the good and evil in all

87

church parties, – who does not see precisely how it is that men have gone wrong hitherto, – and pity philosophers in general that they have not had the opportunity of consulting her. Great writers, who have modestly contented themselves with putting their experience into fiction, and have thought it quite a sufficient task to exhibit men and things as they are, she sighs over as deplorably deficient in the application of their powers. 'They have solved no great questions' – and she is ready to remedy their omission by setting before you a complete theory of life and manual of divinity, in a love story, where ladies and gentlemen of good family go through genteel vicissitudes, to the utter confusion of Deists, Puseyites, and ultra-Protestants, and to the perfect establishment of that particular view of Christianity which either condenses itself into a sentence of small caps, or explodes into a cluster of stars on the three hundred and thirtieth page. It is true, the ladies and gentlemen will probably seem to you remarkably little like any you have had the fortune or misfortune to meet with, for, as a general rule, the ability of a lady novelist to describe actual life and her fellow-men, is in inverse proportion to her confident eloquence about God and the other world, and the means by which she usually chooses to conduct you to true ideas of the invisible is a totally false picture of the visible.

As typical a novel of the oracular kind as we can hope to meet with, is *The Enigma: A Leaf from the Chronicles of*

Wolchorley House. The 'enigma' which this novel is to solve, is certainly one that demands powers no less gigantic than those of a lady novelist, being neither more nor less than the existence of evil. The problem is stated, and the answer dimly foreshadowed on the very first page. The spirited young lady, with raven hair, says, 'All life is an inextricable confusion'; and the meek young lady, with auburn hair, looks at the picture of the Madonna which she is copying, and – '*There* seemed the solution of that mighty enigma.' The style of this novel is quite as lofty as its purpose; indeed, some passages on which we have spent much patient study are quite beyond our reach, in spite of the illustrative aid of italics and small caps; and we must await further 'development' in order to understand them. Of Ernest, the model young clergyman, who sets every one right on all occasions, we read, that 'he held not of marriage in the marketable kind, after a social desecration'; that, on one eventful night, 'sleep had not visited his divided heart, where tumultuated, in varied type and combination, the aggregate feelings of grief and joy'; and that, 'for the *marketable* human article he had no toleration, be it of what sort, or set for what value it might, whether for worship or class, his upright soul abhorred it, whose ultimatum, the self-deceiver, was to him THE *great spiritual lie*, "living in a vain show, deceiving and being deceived"; since he did not suppose the phylactery and enlarged border on the garment to be *merely* a social trick.' (The italics and small caps are the author's, and we hope they assist the reader's comprehension.) Of Sir Lionel, the model old gentleman, we are told that 'the simple ideal of the middle age, apart from its anarchy and decadence, in him most truly seemed to live again, when the ties which knit men together were of heroic cast. The first-born colours of pristine faith and truth engraven on the common soul of man, and blent into the wide arch of brotherhood, where the primæval law of *order* grew and multiplied, each perfect after his kind, and mutually interdependent.' You see clearly, of course, how colours are first engraven on a soul, and then blent into a wide arch, on which arch of colours – apparently a rainbow – the law of order grew and multiplied, each – apparently the arch and the law – perfect after his kind? If, after this, you can possibly want any further aid towards knowing what Sir Lionel was, we can tell you, that in his soul 'the scientific combinations of thought could educe no fuller harmonies of the good and the true, than lay in the primæval pulses which floated as an atmosphere around it!' and that, when he was sealing a letter, 'Lo! the responsive throb in that good man's bosom echoed back in simple truth the honest witness of a heart that condemned him not, as his eye, bedewed with love, rested, too, with something of ancestral pride, on the undimmed motto of the family – LOIAUTÉ.'

The slightest matters have their vulgarity fumigated out of them by the same elevated style. Commonplace people would say that a copy of Shakspeare lay on a drawing-room table; but the authoress of *The Enigma*, bent on edifying periphrasis, tells you that there lay on the table, 'that fund of human thought and feeling, which teaches the heart through the little name, "Shakspeare" '. A watchman sees a light burning in an upper window rather longer than usual, and thinks that people are foolish to sit up late when they have an opportunity of going to bed; but, lest this fact should seem too low and common, it is presented to us in the following striking and metaphysical manner: 'He marvelled – as man *will* think for others in a necessarily separate personality, consequently (though disallowing it) in false mental premise, – how differently *he* should act, how gladly *he* should prize the rest so lightly held of within.' A footman – an ordinary Jeames, with large calves and aspirated vowels – answers the door-bell, and the opportunity is seized to tell you that he was a 'type of the large class of pampered menials, who follow the curse of Cain – "vagabonds" on the face of the earth, and whose estimate of the human class varies in the graduated scale of money and expenditure ... These, and such as these, O England, be the false lights of thy morbid civilization!' We have heard of various 'false lights', from Dr Cumming to Robert Owen, from Dr Pusey to the Spirit-rappers, but we never before heard of the false light that emanates from plush and powder.

In the same way very ordinary events of civilized life are exalted into the most awful crises, and ladies in full skirts and *manches à la chinoise*, conduct themselves not unlike the heroines of sanguinary melodramas.

Mrs Percy, a shallow woman of the world, wishes her son Horace to marry the auburn-haired Grace, she being an heiress; but he, after the manner of sons, falls in love with the raven-haired Kate, the heiress's portionless cousin; and, moreover, Grace herself shows every symptom of perfect indifference to Horace. In such cases, sons are often sulky or fiery, mothers are alternately manœuvring and waspish, and the portionless young lady often lies awake at night and cries a good deal. We are getting used to these things now, just as we are used to eclipses of the moon, which no longer set us howling and beating tin kettles. We never heard of a lady in a fashionable 'front' behaving like Mrs Percy under these circumstances. Happening one day to see Horace talking to Grace at a window, without in the least knowing what they are talking about, or having the least reason to believe that Grace, who is mistress of the house and a person of dignity, would accept her son if he were to offer himself, she suddenly rushes up to them and clasps them both, saying, 'with a flushed countenance and in an excited manner' – 'This is indeed happiness; for, may I not call you so, Grace? – my Grace – my Horace's Grace! – my dear children!' Her son tells her she is mistaken, and that he is engaged to Kate, whereupon we have the following scene and tableau: –

Gathering herself up to an unprecedented height, (!) her eyes lightning forth the fire of her anger: –

'Wretched boy!' she said, hoarsely and scornfully, and clenching her hand. 'Take then the doom of your own choice! Bow down your miserable head and let a mother's –'

'Curse not!' spake a deep low voice from behind, and Mrs Percy started, scared, as though she had seen a heavenly visitant appear, to break upon her in the midst of her sin.

Meantime, Horace had fallen on his knees at her feet, and hid his face in his hands.

Who, then, is she – who! Truly his 'guardian spirit' hath stepped between him and the fearful words, which, however unmerited, must have hung as a pall over his future existence; – a spell which could not be unbound – which could not be unsaid.

Of an earthly paleness, but calm with the still, iron-bound calmness of death – the only calm one there, – Katherine stood; and her words smote on the ear in tones whose appallingly slow and separate intonation rung on the heart like the chill, isolated tolling of some fatal knell.

'He would have plighted me his faith, but I did not accept it; you cannot, therefore – you *dare* not curse him. And here,' she continued, raising her hand to heaven, whither her large dark eyes also rose with a chastened glow, which, for the first time, *suffering* had lighted in those passionate orbs, – 'here I promise, come weal, come woe, that Horace Wolchorley and I do never interchange vows without his mother's sanction – without his mother's blessing!'

Here, and throughout the story, we see that confusion of purpose which is so characteristic of silly novels written by women. It is a story of quite modern drawing-room society – a society in which polkas are played and Puseyism discussed; yet we have characters, and incidents, and traits of manner introduced, which are mere shreds from the most heterogeneous romances. We have a blind Irish harper, 'relic of the picturesque bards of yore', startling us at a Sunday-school festival of tea and cake in an English village; we have a crazy gypsy, in a scarlet cloak, singing snatches of romantic song, and revealing a secret on her death-bed which, with the testimony of a dwarfish miserly merchant, who salutes strangers with a curse and a devilish laugh, goes to prove that Ernest, the model young clergyman, is Kate's brother; and we have an ultra-virtuous Irish Barney, discovering that a document is forged, by comparing the date of the paper with the date of the alleged signature, although the same document has passed through a court of law, and occasioned a fatal decision. The 'Hall' in which Sir Lionel lives is the venerable country-seat of an old family, and this, we suppose, sets the imagination of the authoress flying to donjons and battlements, where 'lo! the warder blows his horn'; for, as the inhabitants are in their bedrooms on a night certainly within the recollection of Pleaceman X., and a breeze springs up, which we are at first told was faint, and then that it made the old cedars bow their branches to the greensward, she falls into this mediæval vein of description (the italics are ours): 'The banner *unfurled it* at the sound, and shook its guardian wing above, while the startled owl *flapped her* in the ivy; the firmament looking down through her "argus eyes" –

> Ministers of heaven's mute melodies.

And lo! two strokes tolled from out the warder tower, and "Two o'clock" re-echoed its interpreter below.'

Such stories as this of *The Enigma* remind us of the pictures clever children sometimes draw 'out of their own head', where you will see a modern villa on the right, two knights in helmets fighting in the foreground, and a tiger grinning in a jungle on the left, the several objects being brought together because the artist thinks each pretty, and perhaps still more because he remembers seeing them in other pictures.

But we like the authoress much better on her mediæval stilts than on her oracular ones, – when she talks of the *Ich* and of 'subjective' and 'objective', and lays down the exact line of Christian verity, between 'right-hand excesses and left-hand declensions'. Persons who deviate from this line are introduced with a patronizing air of charity. Of a certain Miss Inshquine she informs us, with all the lucidity of italics and small caps, that '*function*, not *form*, AS THE INEVITABLE OUTER EXPRESSION OF THE SPIRIT IN THIS TABERNACLED AGE, weakly engrossed her'. And *à propos* of Miss Mayjar, an evangelical lady who is a little too apt to talk of her visits to sick women and the state of their souls, we are told that the model clergyman is 'not one to disallow, through the *super* crust, the undercurrent towards good in the *subject*, or the positive benefits, nevertheless, to the *object*'. We imagine the double-refined accent and protrusion of chin which are feebly represented by the italics in this lady's sentences. We abstain from quoting any of her oracular doctrinal passages, because they refer to matters too serious for our pages just now.

The epithet 'silly' may seem impertinent, applied to a novel which indicates so much reading and intellectual activity as *The Enigma*; but we use this epithet advisedly. If, as the world has long agreed, a very great amount of instruction will not make a wise man, still less will a very mediocre amount of instruction make a wise woman. And the most mischievous form of feminine silliness is the literary form, because it tends to confirm the popular prejudice against the more solid education of women. When men see girls wasting their time in consultations about bonnets and ball dresses, and in giggling or sentimental love-confidences, or middle-aged women mismanaging their children, and solacing themselves with acrid gossip, they can hardly help saying, 'For Heaven's sake, let girls be better educated; let them have some better objects of thought – some more solid occupations.' But after a few hours' conversation with an oracular literary woman, or a few hours' reading of her books, they are likely enough to say, 'After all, when a woman gets

some knowledge, see what use she makes of it! Her
knowledge remains acquisition, instead of passing into
culture; instead of being subdued into modesty and sim-
plicity by a larger acquaintance with thought and fact,
she has a feverish consciousness of her attainments; she
keeps a sort of mental pocket-mirror, and is continually
looking in it at her own 'intellectuality'; she spoils the
taste of one's muffin by questions of metaphysics; 'puts
down' men at a dinner-table with her superior information; and seizes the opportunity of a *soirée* to catechize
us on the vital question of the relation between mind and
matter. And then, look at her writings! She mistakes
vagueness for depth, bombast for eloquence, and affectation for originality; she struts on one page, rolls her eyes
on another, grimaces in a third, and is hysterical in a
fourth. She may have read many writings of great men,
and a few writings of great women; but she is as unable
to discern the difference between her own style and theirs
as a Yorkshireman is to discern the difference between
his own English and a Londoner's: rhodomontade is the
native accent of her intellect. No – the average nature of
women is too shallow and feeble a soil to bear much till-
age; it is only fit for the very lightest crops.'

It is true that the men who come to such a decision on
such very superficial and imperfect observation may not
be among the wisest in the world; but we have not now
to contest their opinion – we are only pointing out how
it is unconsciously encouraged by many women who have

97

volunteered themselves as representatives of the feminine intellect. We do not believe that a man was ever strengthened in such an opinion by associating with a woman of true culture, whose mind had absorbed her knowledge instead of being absorbed by it. A really cultured woman, like a really cultured man, is all the simpler and the less obtrusive for her knowledge; it has made her see herself and her opinions in something like just proportions; she does not make it a pedestal from which she flatters herself that she commands a complete view of men and things, but makes it a point of observation from which to form a right estimate of herself. She neither spouts poetry nor quotes Cicero on slight provocation; not because she thinks that a sacrifice must be made to the prejudices of men, but because that mode of exhibiting her memory and Latinity does not present itself to her as edifying or graceful. She does not write books to confound philosophers, perhaps because she is able to write books that delight them. In conversation she is the least formidable of women, because she understands you, without wanting to make you aware that you *can't* understand her. She does not give you information, which is the raw material of culture, – she gives you sympathy, which is its subtlest essence.

A more numerous class of silly novels than the oracular, (which are generally inspired by some form of High Church, or transcendental Christianity,) is what we may call the *white neck-cloth* species, which represent the tone of thought and feeling in the Evangelical party. This species is a kind of genteel tract on a large scale, intended as a sort of medicinal sweetmeat for Low Church young ladies; an Evangelical substitute for the fashionable novel, as the May Meetings are a substitute for the Opera. Even Quaker children, one would think, can hardly have been denied the indulgence of a doll; but it must be a doll dressed in a drab gown and a coal-scuttle bonnet – not a worldly doll, in gauze and spangles. And there are no young ladies, we imagine, – unless they belong to the Church of the United Brethren, in which people are married without any love-making – who can dispense with love stories. Thus, for Evangelical young ladies there are Evangelical love stories, in which the vicissitudes of the tender passion are sanctified by saving views of Regeneration and the Atonement. These novels differ from the oracular ones, as a Low Churchwoman often differs from a High Churchwoman: they are a little less supercilious, and a great deal more ignorant, a little less correct in their syntax, and a great deal more vulgar.

The Orlando of Evangelical literature is the young curate, looked at from the point of view of the middle class, where cambric bands are understood to have as thrilling an effect on the hearts of young ladies as epaulettes have in the classes above and below it. In the ordinary type of these novels, the hero is almost sure to be a young curate, frowned upon, perhaps, by worldly mammas, but carrying captive the hearts of their daughters, who can 'never forget *that* sermon'; tender glances are seized from the pulpit stairs instead of the opera-box; *tête-à-têtes* are seasoned with quotations from Scripture, instead of quotations from the poets; and questions as to the state of the heroine's affections are mingled with anxieties as to the state of her soul. The young curate always has a background of well-dressed and wealthy, if not fashionable society; – for Evangelical silliness is as snobbish as any other kind of silliness; and the Evangelical lady novelist, while she explains to you the type of the scapegoat on one page, is ambitious on another to represent the manners and conversation of aristocratic people. Her pictures of fashionable society are often curious studies considered as efforts of the Evangelical imagination; but in one particular the novels of the White Neck-cloth School are meritoriously realistic, – their favourite hero, the Evangelical young curate, is always rather an insipid personage.

The most recent novel of this species that we happen to have before us, is *The Old Grey Church*. It is utterly tame and feeble; there is no one set of objects on which the writer seems to have a stronger grasp than on any other; and we should be entirely at a loss to conjecture among what phases of life her experience has been gained, but for certain vulgarisms of style which sufficiently indicate that she has had the advantage, though she has been unable to use it, of mingling chiefly with men and women whose manners and characters have not had all their bosses and angles rubbed down by refined conventionalism. It is less excusable in an Evangelical novelist, than in any other, gratuitously to seek her subjects among titles and carriages. The real drama of Evangelicalism – and it has abundance of fine drama for any one who has genius enough to discern and reproduce it – lies among the middle and lower classes; and are not Evangelical opinions understood to give an especial interest in the weak things of the earth, rather than in the mighty? Why then, cannot our Evangelical lady novelists show us the operation of their religious views among people (there really are many such in the world) who keep no carriage, 'not so much as a brass-bound gig', who even manage to eat their dinner without a silver fork, and in whose mouths the authoress's questionable English would be strictly consistent? Why can we not have pictures of religious life among the industrial classes in England, as interesting as Mrs Stowe's pictures of religious life among the negroes? Instead of this, pious ladies nauseate us with novels which remind us of what we sometimes see in a worldly woman recently 'converted'; – she is as fond of a fine dinner table as before, but she invites clergymen instead of beaux; she thinks as much of her dress as before, but she adopts a more sober choice of colours and patterns; her conversation is as trivial as before, but the triviality is flavoured with Gospel instead of gossip. In *The Old Grey Church*, we have the same sort of Evangelical travesty of the fashionable novel, and of course the vicious, intriguing baronet is not wanting. It is worth while to give a sample of the style of conversation attributed to this high-born rake – a style that in its profuse italics and palpable innuendoes, is worthy of Miss Squeers. In an evening visit to the ruins of the Colosseum, Eustace, the young clergyman, has been withdrawing the heroine, Miss Lushington, from the rest of the party, for the sake of a *tête-à-tête*. The baronet is jealous, and vents his pique in this way: –

> There they are, and Miss Lushington, no doubt, quite safe; for she is under the holy guidance of Pope Eustace the First, who has, of course, been delivering to her an edifying homily on the wickedness of the heathens of yore, who, as tradition tells us, in this very place let loose the wild *beasties* on poor Saint Paul! – Oh, no! by the bye, I believe I am wrong, and betraying my want of clergy, and that it was not at all Saint Paul, nor was it here. But no matter, it would equally serve as a text to preach from, and from which to diverge to the degenerate *heathen* Christians of the present day, and all their naughty practices, and so end with an exhortation to 'come out from among them, and be separate'; – and I am sure, Miss Lushington, you have most scrupulously conformed to that injunction this evening, for we have seen nothing of you since our arrival. But every one seems agreed it has been a *charming party of pleasure*, and I am sure we all feel *much indebted* to Mr Grey for having *suggested* it; and as he seems so capital a cicerone,

I hope he will think of something else equally agreeable to *all*.

This drivelling kind of dialogue, and equally drivelling narrative, which, like a bad drawing, represents nothing, and barely indicates what is meant to be represented, runs through the book; and we have no doubt is considered by the amiable authoress to constitute an improving novel, which Christian mothers will do well to put into the hands of their daughters. But everything is relative; we have met with American vegetarians whose normal diet was dry meal, and who, when their appetite wanted stimulating, tickled it with *wet* meal; and so, we can imagine that there are Evangelical circles in which *The Old Grey Church* is devoured as a powerful and interesting fiction.

But, perhaps, the least readable of silly women's novels, are the *modern-antique* species, which unfold to us the domestic life of Jannes and Jambres, the private love affairs of Sennacherib, or the mental struggles and ultimate conversion of Demetrius the silversmith. From most silly novels we can at least extract a laugh; but those of the modern-antique school have a ponderous, a leaden kind of fatuity, under which we groan. What can be more demonstrative of the inability of literary women to measure their own powers, than their frequent assumption of a task which can only be justified by the rarest concurrence of acquirement with genius? The finest effort to reanimate the past is of course only approximative – is always more or less an infusion of the modern spirit into the ancient form, –

> Was ihr den Geist der Zeiten heisst,
> Das ist im Grund der Herren eigner Geist,
> In dem die Zeiten sich bespiegeln.*

Admitting that genius which has familiarized itself with all the relics of an ancient period can sometimes, by the force of its sympathetic divination, restore the missing notes in the 'music of humanity', and reconstruct the fragments into a whole which will really bring the remote past nearer to us, and interpret it to our duller apprehension, – this form of imaginative power must always be among the very rarest, because it demands as much accurate and minute knowledge as creative vigour. Yet we find ladies constantly choosing to make their mental mediocrity more conspicuous, by clothing it in a masquerade of ancient names; by putting their feeble sentimentality into the mouths of Roman vestals or Egyptian princesses, and attributing their rhetorical arguments to Jewish high-priests and Greek philosophers. A recent example of this heavy imbecility is *Adonijah, a Tale of the Jewish Dispersion*, which forms part of a series, 'uniting,' we are told, 'taste,

---

*   'What you call the spirit of the age
      Is but the critic's spirit, in whose page
      The age itself is darkly glassed.'

humour, and sound principles'. *Adonijah*, we presume, exemplifies the tale of 'sound principles'; the taste and humour are to be found in other members of the series. We are told on the cover, that the incidents of this tale are 'fraught with unusual interest', and the preface winds up thus: 'To those who feel interested in the dispersed of Israel and Judea, these pages may afford, perhaps, information on an important subject, as well as amusement'. Since the 'important subject' on which this book is to afford information is not specified, it may possibly lie in some esoteric meaning to which we have no key; but if it has relation to the dispersed of Israel and Judea at any period of their history, we believe a tolerably well-informed school-girl already knows much more of it than she will find in this 'Tale of the Jewish Dispersion'. *Adonijah* is simply the feeblest kind of love story, supposed to be instructive, we presume, because the hero is a Jewish captive, and the heroine a Roman vestal; because they and their friends are converted to Christianity after the shortest and easiest method approved by the 'Society for Promoting the Conversion of the Jews'; and because, instead of being written in plain language, it is adorned with that peculiar style of grandiloquence which is held by some lady novelists to give an antique colouring; and which we recognize at once in such phrases as these: – 'the splendid regnal talents undoubtedly possessed by the Emperor Nero' – 'the expiring scion of a lofty stem' – 'the virtuous partner of his couch' – 'ah, by

Vesta!' – and 'I tell thee, Roman'. Among the quotations which serve at once for instruction and ornament on the cover of this volume, there is one from Miss Sinclair, which informs us that 'Works of imagination are *avowedly* read by men of science, wisdom, and piety'; from which we suppose the reader is to gather the cheering inference that Dr Daubeny, Mr Mill, or Mr Maurice, may openly indulge himself with the perusal of *Adonijah*, without being obliged to secrete it among the sofa cushions, or read it by snatches under the dinner-table.

'Be not a baker if your head be made of butter,' says a homely proverb, which, being interpreted, may mean, let no woman rush into print who is not prepared for the consequences. We are aware that our remarks are in a very different tone from that of the reviewers who, with a perennial recurrence of precisely similar emotions, only paralleled, we imagine, in the experience of monthly nurses, tell one lady novelist after another that they 'hail' her productions 'with delight'. We are aware that the ladies at whom our criticism is pointed are accustomed to be told, in the choicest phraseology of puffery, that their pictures of life are brilliant, their characters well-drawn, their style fascinating, and their sentiments lofty. But if they are inclined to resent our plainness of speech, we ask them to reflect for a moment on the chary praise, and often captious blame, which their panegyrists give to writers whose works are on the way to become classics.

No sooner does a woman show that she has genius or effective talent, than she receives the tribute of being moderately praised and severely criticized. By a peculiar thermometric adjustment, when a woman's talent is at zero, journalistic approbation is at the boiling pitch; when she attains mediocrity, it is already at no more than summer heat; and if ever she reaches excellence, critical enthusiasm drops to the freezing point. Harriet Martineau, Currer Bell, and Mrs Gaskell have been treated as cavalierly as if they had been men. And every critic who forms a high estimate of the share women may ultimately take in literature, will, on principle, abstain from any exceptional indulgence towards the productions of literary women. For it must be plain to every one who looks impartially and extensively into feminine literature, that its greatest deficiencies are due hardly more to the want of intellectual power than to the want of those moral qualities that contribute to literary excellence – patient diligence, a sense of the responsibility involved in publication, and an appreciation of the sacredness of the writer's art. In the majority of women's books you see that kind of facility which springs from the absence of any high standard; that fertility in imbecile combination or feeble imitation which a little self-criticism would check and reduce to barrenness; just as with a total want of musical ear people will sing out of tune, while a degree more melodic sensibility would suffice to render them silent. The foolish vanity of wishing to appear in print, instead of being counterbalanced by any consciousness of the intellectual or moral derogation implied in futile authorship, seems to be encouraged by the extremely false impression that to write *at all* is a proof of superiority in a woman. On this ground, we believe that the average intellect of women is unfairly represented by the mass of feminine literature, and that while the few women who write well are very far above the ordinary intellectual level of their sex, the many women who write ill are very far below it. So that, after all, the severer critics are fulfilling a chivalrous duty in depriving the mere fact of feminine authorship of any false prestige which may give it a delusive attraction, and in recommending women of mediocre faculties – as at least a negative service they can render their sex – to abstain from writing.

The standing apology for women who become writers without any special qualification is, that society shuts them out from other spheres of occupation. Society is a very culpable entity, and has to answer for the manufacture of many unwholesome commodities, from bad pickles to bad poetry. But society, like 'matter', and Her Majesty's Government, and other lofty abstractions, has its share of excessive blame as well as excessive praise. Where there is one woman who writes from necessity, we believe there are three women who write from vanity; and, besides, there is something so antiseptic in the mere healthy fact of working for one's bread, that the most trashy and rotten kind of feminine literature is not likely to have been produced under such circumstances. 'In all labour there is profit'; but ladies' silly novels, we imagine, are less the result of labour than of busy idleness.

Happily, we are not dependent on argument to prove that Fiction is a department of literature in which women can, after their kind, fully equal men. A cluster of great names, both living and dead, rush to our memories in evidence that women can produce novels not only fine, but among the very finest; – novels, too, that have a precious speciality, lying quite apart from masculine aptitudes and experience. No educational restrictions can shut women out from the materials of fiction, and there is no species of art which is so free from rigid requirements. Like crystalline masses, it may take any form, and yet be beautiful; we have only to pour in the right elements – genuine observation, humour, and passion. But it is precisely this absence of rigid requirement which constitutes the fatal seduction of novel-writing to incompetent women. Ladies are not wont to be very grossly deceived as to their power of playing on the piano; here certain positive difficulties of execution have to be conquered, and incompetence inevitably breaks down. Every art which has its absolute *technique* is, to a certain extent, guarded from the intrusions of mere left-handed imbecility. But in novel-writing there are no barriers for incapacity to stumble against, no external criteria to prevent a writer from mistaking foolish facility for mastery. And so we have again and again the old story of

La Fontaine's ass, who puts his nose to the flute, and, finding that he elicits some sound, exclaims, 'Moi, aussi, je joue de la flute'; – a fable which we commend, at parting, to the consideration of any feminine reader who is in danger of adding to the number of 'silly novels by lady novelists'.